Also by this Author...

Governess In Love

Charlotte Blythe is a gifted young governess, but when falsely accused and disgraced, she is forced to take a position in the house of broken and brooding politician, Thomas Mallory.

Can Charlotte and Thomas find their way through a quagmire of lies and subterfuge to find their second chances?

Chambermaid In Love

Florence Watson and her unborn baby are destined for the workhouse when she is rescued by the mysterious Edwin Thackeray, an academic who likes to collect beautiful things. But why has Edwin rescued her, and what does he have in mind? Florence begins to fear that there are worse fates than destitution.

Romantic Herald

Flower Girl in Love

ELIZABETH LOVETT-BELL

Flower Girl in Love

Copyright © 2024 by Elizabeth Lovett-Bell.

All Rights Reserved.

All rights reserved. No part of this book may be reproduced in any form or by any electronic or mechanical means including information storage and retrieval systems, without permission in writing from the author. The only exception is by a reviewer, who may quote short excerpts in a review.

This book is a work of fiction. Names, characters, places, and incidents either are products of the author's imagination or are used fictitiously. Any resemblance to actual persons, living or dead, events, or locales is entirely coincidental.

ISBN: 9798338014011

Acknowledgement

To My Mother

Romantic Herald

Contents

1. Chapter One — 1
2. Chapter Two — 15
3. Chapter Three — 26
4. Chapter Four — 34
5. Chapter Five — 44
6. Chapter Six — 57
7. Chapter Seven — 67
8. Chapter Eight — 80
9. Chapter Nine — 92
10. Chapter Ten — 103

Note from the author — 113

Chapter One

Twelve-year-old Sparrow came leaping through the crowded market. His thin white face with terrified eyes that seemed altogether too large for his head, kept appearing and disappearing over the top of the crowds like a meerkat.

"Rosie! They're coming for us!" Sparrow's frantic yells were lost over the clamour of the stall holders.

Sparrow scrambled under stalls and through legs and buckets until he reached the poor end of the market; the end where there were no stalls but only barrows. "They're going to kill us this time most certainly," wailed the boy squeezing through the wheels of Rosie Potter's flower barrow to reach the cart where he sold his beloved birds.

Sparrow put a protective arm around the little cane cages where he kept his collection of home bred finches. "You said Arthur would come," he moaned accusingly. "Where is he? They're going to kill us this time. They'll kill my birds and then they'll kill us!"

The other barrow vendors turned panic-stricken faces to Rosie, the girl who despite her tender nineteen years of age always knew what to do and what to say.

Rosie twisted the cheap brass engagement ring on her finger. Subconsciously, she tried to get the little paste diamond to catch the light, but it had been on her finger so long that it had grown black.

"Arthur will come," said Rosie stoutly. "He said he would be here, and he will be here." She looked across the sea of colourful market awnings to the colonnades of the indoor market and its flight of steep steps. The Heneghan brothers were emerging from the indoor market and descending into the outdoor stalls. There were five of them, stockily built and wearing suits that did nothing to disguise their profession as self-appointed protection racketeers.

"And if Arthur for some reason doesn't come," said Rosie, her loyalty wavering, "we will fight them ourselves."

Without having to look round, Rosie could sense the horror of her fellow barrow vendors.

"I don't know about that," said Ma' Maggie who was turning chestnuts on a hot griddle. "I'm too old to fight. I think maybe we should pay the protection money."

There was a murmur of agreement from behind the other barrows. "Yes, let's pay the protection money this time."

Rosie tossed her long glossy red curls and put her hands on her hips in a gesture of defiance. "Is that what you all want?" she challenged. "Sparrow, you've been breeding your finches since you were knee high. Are you going to hand over your hard-earned profit?" She turned her attention to the twelve-year-old twins, Charlie and Will. "And you," she said. "What are you going to tell your ma'? She's been up half the night baking those pastries to sell. What are you going to tell her when there's no brass to take home?"

The twins glanced at each other uncomfortably. It was true. Their mother had worked half the night to fill the pastry baskets for the barrow. What would she say if she was to learn that the Heneghan brothers had walked off with all their earnings?

"What about you Eddie?" Rosie spoke in a gentler tone to the eleven-year-old boy whose body was buckled with palsy and unable to speak. "You spend hours on the river catching fresh eels to sell." She picked up the tin in which Eddie kept his money and shook it. "This is your money not the Heneghans'. It is you who has spent long hours on the river not the Heneghans. Why should they walk off with what you have earned?"

Ma' Maggie heaped more chestnuts into newspaper cones. "I suppose Rosie is right," she said at length. "We have to fight."

"But how?" wailed Sparrow. "They're bigger than us and they have weapons."

Rosie thought fast. She didn't know what she was going to do but she knew something would come to her. All she knew was that she had to protect her friends. They were more than friends to her. She had come to regard them as family. She bobbed down to Sparrow's level. "Listen carefully," she said. "Run as fast as you can to Leadbetter and Weightman's on Lombard Wynd. Ask for Arthur Tipple. Tell him that he must come as fast as he can."

Sparrow nodded and shot off into the crowd.

Rosie turned to the others and ordered them to stand behind her. "Stand firm," she said. "Follow my lead."

The Heneghans pushed through the crowds their eyes darting left and right on the look-out for their most vulnerable prey. Morgan Heneghan, the brothers' self-appointed leader, spotted the twins on their pastry barrow. His face broke into a sadistic smile.

"What do we have here?" said Morgan nastily, and he helped himself to a pastry and crammed it into his mouth leaving flakes stuck in his unkempt beard.

"Here!" cried Charlie. "You pay for that mister."

"Or what?" laughed Morgan Heneghan with his mouth full. He grabbed Charlie's cravat and lifted the child off the ground. "I think you'll find it's you that owes me." He looked round at the little group of terrified vendors. "That goes for all of you. Time to pay up!"

"Or what?" challenged Rosie. She stepped up to Morgan Heneghan with her arms crossed and looked up into his pot-marked face her mouth set in an obstinate line.

Morgan Heneghan regarded her for a moment. Then he opened his jacket and pulled out a wooden club. "Or this!" He lashed out at Rosie's flower barrow with unbridled violence. One of the wheels twisted and the barrow tipped. A flower basket crashed, and its contents spilled across the cobbles. Morgan Heneghan stamped on the fallen violets and daisies and crushed them under his boot. "Oh dear!" he said. "That's a shame ain't it?" He looked round nastily. "Anyone ready to pay up?" His eyes settled on Eddie and his eyes narrowed nastily. "What about you?" Morgan advanced with threat in every sinew. He aimed his boot cruelly and kicked the child's little wooden crutch from beneath him. Eddie fell to his knees and shrank back in terror.

The little gang of vendors looked to Rosie. Surely, they were no match for the Heneghan brothers. Rosie looked from Eddie's terrified little face to her broken barrow and back to the Heneghans' sneering faces and she was overcome by a rage she'd never known before. In a trice she grabbed the large chestnut pan from Ma' Maggie's stall. Tipping hot chestnuts onto the ground she swung the pan with all her might in Morgan Heneghan's direction. The pan struck Morgan's arm hard, and he fell to the ground howling in pain.

"Who's next?" asked Rosie sweetly.

"Get her!" roared Morgan struggling to get up. "Get her! Make her sorry!"

The Heneghan brothers drew weapons and advanced. Will and Charlie grabbed broom handles and ran to Rosie's defence. Eddie struggled to his feet and grabbed an empty bucket in one hand and a plank in the other. Rosie swung the pan wildly from left to right. "You won't get another ha'penny out of us for your so-called protection!" she yelled.

The Heneghans hesitated. They weren't used to being challenged.

"What are you waiting for?" Morgan waved his brothers on. "They're a bunch of kids, a waif of a girl and an old woman. We'll be a laughing stock if we let 'em off." Then he aimed a blow which caught Rosie on her chin and sent her sprawling. For a second or two her world span. She was aware that crowds were gathering but nobody seemed inclined to help. It was as if the fate of some poor barrow vendors was of no consequence.

It seemed that all was lost, when as if by some miracle, a tall lean man leapt onto the scene as if from nowhere. He was dressed poorly but there was no wastage in his muscular arms and fists. He dealt the unsuspecting Morgan Heneghan a punch that sent him reeling. The Heneghan brothers rounded on the newcomer their weapons raised in attack. The man reacted with lightning speed. His fists and feet were a blur as he disarmed the attackers and dodged their fists. He leapt up onto a crate and used it as springboard to land a powerful kick into Morgan's chest. The crowds began to cheer as though it was entertainment. Rosie stood and gaped. She had never seen a man fight as impressively as this. The man was unstoppable. He weaved through the ensuing chaos dealing blow after blow with unerring accuracy and incredible force. Realising that they were out-classed, Morgan gestured to his brothers to retreat. "I'll be back Rosie Potter," shouted Morgan over his shoulder. "We will make you very sorry!"

Rosie was sitting on the cobbles rubbing her aching jaw. "Come back if you want," she shouted back. "We'll be ready for you!"

Sparrow reappeared looking back in puzzlement at the retreating Heneghans. "Couldn't find Arthur," he panted. "Leadbetter and Weightman's said it wasn't his day."

"Not his day?" repeated Rosie blankly. "No matter. Turns out we didn't need him after all."

The little group of vendors helped each other put their barrows back in order.

Ma' Maggie meanwhile was watching their mystery rescuer as he limped off into the crowd. "Rosie Potter," she said. "Get after that man and find out who he is. We'll be needing him again most likely."

Rosie charged through the crowds pushing her flower barrow as fast as she could. The broken wheel jarred and tipped on the jagged cobbles making progress hard. Ahead of her she could see the mysterious rescuer disappearing through the crowds and out into the labyrinth of streets beyond. If she didn't hurry, she would lose him.

"Sir, wait!" Rosie shouted. She wondered why she should be addressing a man in rags as 'sir'. There was something about his height and confident gait that commanded deference. "Sir!" she shouted again. "Wait!"

The man stopped and turned his head. Puffing and panting at the effort of pushing a broken barrow, Rosie managed to catch him up.

"Sir," she said wondering what to say to him now that she had caught him up. "We wondered wherever you learned to fight like that. We wanted to thank you."

He looked down at her with a faint smile. "I can't abide bullies," he said. "It did my soul good to see those thugs on the run."

Rosie grinned. "It did my soul good too," she said. Suddenly shy, she offered her hand. "I'm Rosie," she said. "Rosie Potter."

He hesitated to accept her handshake, then he took her hand firmly in his. "Jack," he returned.

She looked down in horror at his knuckles. They were covered in blood. "You're hurt," she said. Then she glanced up into his face. "And your eye!" she gasped.

"One of our friends was carrying a knife," said Jack holding his sleeve to stem the blood from a gash above his left eye.

"Follow me," said Rosie authoritatively. "I live two streets away. I'll clean and bandage your cuts."

Rosie grabbed the handles of her barrow and headed off. She didn't look round to check that Jack was following her. Although only nineteen years old, she had learned that people tended not to disobey her. She didn't register the surprise nor the flicker of amusement that crossed Jack's bloodied face.

He caught her up. "If you're going to give me water and bandages, at least let me push the barrow." He took the handles from her and pushed the barrow as though it weighed nothing at all.

They walked along in companionable silence for a moment or two. Rosie was aware of what a typical couple they must look, she in her faded blue calico dress and Jack in a patchwork of mended fabric. She smiled to herself. They might look to every passer-by like a typical couple, but she knew deep down that she was no typical flower seller. She was going to marry Arthur Tipple, and when she was Mrs Tipple, she would trade the faded calico for embroidered silk and fine bonnets.

"Do the Heneghan brothers call every month?" asked Jack cutting across her fantasy.

Rosie nodded with a slight frown. Did she know Jack well enough yet to ask if he would come and protect the little band of barrow vendors every month?

"Why don't you report it to the police?" said Jack.

Rosie threw him an astonished look. "You're not from round here are you?" she laughed. "Do you imagine for one moment that the likes of Eddie or Ma' Maggie or Sparrow has a barrow licence? Folks round here have more to fear from the police than from the protection racketeers."

The lamp lighter was making his way from street to street, and the eerie glow of the gas lights reflected in the wet cobbles. Rosie stopped and waved her hand at an end terrace. "Here we are," she said. "It ain't much but it's mine. Stay here a minute. I'll park the barrow round the back."

Jack looked up at the once red brick house now blackened by soot. The ground floor windows bore iron grills. Tattered lace curtains punctuated the upper windows. Rosie hitched up her apron and produced a key from her pocket. She pushed the barrow through a large wooden gate at the side of the building into a back yard and came through the house from the back yard to let Jack in. She lit a candle and guided Jack into the kitchen. Jack looked all around him. It was a house Rosie had done her best to keep clean, but it smelt of damp and rot.

"Sit by the fire," she ordered. "I'll have it lit in a moment." She tipped a few pieces of coal and kindling from a scuttle and set about lighting a fire.

"Your scuttle's nearly empty," Jack commented. "Do you want me to fetch more coal from the bunker?"

"Bunker?" laughed Rosie shielding a match from the draft with the palm of her hand. "You're really not from round here. Folks round here have to find coal where they can. They don't have bunkers."

"You don't buy it then?" asked Jack.

Rosie gave him a cunning look. "Why buy it when it can be found for free?" she said. "I'm resourceful me. I go down to the wharf when the coal barges come in. There's always some spilt." She held a sheet of newspaper against the grate and the flames roared, transforming the drab room into a cheery haven. "Now then. I'll fetch some water and bandages, and we'll see to these cuts."

Rosie sat on a stool and carefully bathed and bandaged Jack's knuckles. She deftly wound the bandages around his fingers and thumb. Her head was bent in frowning concentration.

Jack looked at her down bent head curiously. "Do you live here all alone?" he asked.

She nodded, tearing the end of the bandage with her teeth and tying a neat knot.

"It's a big house for someone of your age to own," he observed.

She looked up at him sharply. "As I say," she said. "I'm resourceful."

"Were you left it?" he asked.

"You ask rather too many questions," she said and set about bathing his eye.

He winced at the salt solution. "I didn't mean to pry," he said aware that he had hit a nerve.

"What about you?" said Rosie changing the subject. "Where do you live?"

Jack shrugged. "Nowhere," he said. "Wherever I can lay my head."

Rosie frowned. "It's cold to be sleeping rough," she said. She finished bandaging his eye and sat back to admire her handiwork. "I have a stable in my back yard with a loft above it where a stable boy used to sleep. It has a little wooden bed, and I could find you some cushions. It will do you very well until you find somewhere to live."

Jack cast her a look she couldn't read. Something gave her the uncomfortable feeling that she amused him. Nor did it escape her attention that he didn't thank her for the offer of the stable loft, but then, he was most likely a very proud man.

"I will leave you to go and see if the loft is to your liking," she said. "My fiancé is calling for his tea and it might be better if you are not here when he arrives."

Understanding that he was being dismissed, Jack got to his feet and gave a polite nod.

"Thank you Rosie Potter," he said. "You have a shown me kindness I've never known. I hope I can repay you one day."

Rosie washed at the scullery sink and brushed her hair loose. Then she set about cooking a meal. Friday night was Arthur's night. She chopped carrots and potatoes and threw them into a pot. Then she took the oxtails she had been marinating in herbs and added them to the pot too. In no time at all the broth filled the room with a mouth-watering aroma. Rosie set the table with a mis-match of china, her best teapot, and the flowers that Arthur had bought her on his last visit. She took off her apron and waited. She heard the Bow Bells chime eight and then nine. The candle began to burn low, and she lit another one. She went to the window and looked out as though this might hurry Arthur's arrival. A few drunkards were wobbling their way down the street their top hats askew and laughing wildly at some bawdy joke. Rosie was swamped in disappointment. It was clear that Arthur was not going to call.

From the yard at the back came the sound of gentle hammering. Puzzled, Rosie took the candle from the kitchen table and went to look out of the scullery window. By the light of the gas lamp that overlooked the back yard, she saw that Jack was on his hands and knees mending the broken wheel on the flower barrow. Rosie felt a wave of surprise and gratitude. She wasn't used to random acts of kindness, and it had made her fiercely independent. She opened the scullery door and looked out.

Jack looked up at her and wiped the grime from his forehead with the back of his sleeve. "It's lucky that the spokes weren't smashed," he said. "The wheel was hanging off its axle. All fixed now."

Rosie looked at him for a long moment. "Would you like to come in for a bowl of broth?" she asked.

He looked taken aback. "But you're expecting your fiancé." His eyes travelled through the open scullery door to the cheerful kitchen beyond. He looked tempted. He looked like he hadn't eaten in a while.

"Well it appears Arthur is not able to call this evening after all," she said matter-of-factly. "It would be a shame for the broth to waste."

"Yes," he agreed. "It would be a shame for the broth to waste." He returned the mallet to the hook in the stable and followed Rosie through to the kitchen.

"Wash your hands," Rosie indicated the scullery sink like a bossy parent.

Jack raised his eyebrows in sharp amusement. He washed his hands and sat at the kitchen table. Rosie couldn't help observing that he filled Arthur's chair with a far greater presence than Arthur did. She filled two bowls of broth and cut some generous slices of crusty bread.

"Oxtail," noted Jack approvingly. "You eat well."

"Only on a Friday," she confessed.

"For your fiancé's sake?"

"Yes, Friday night is 'Arthur's night',"

"But he's not here."

"No," said Rosie. "He's not always able to call. Sometimes his work involves travel to see new clients. He's not always able to let me know."

"He has an important job then," said Jack eyeing her curiously. "What does he do?"

"He's a trainee accountant for Leadbetter and Weightman's on Lombard Wynd," said Rosie proudly.

"A trainee?" quizzed Jack. "Is it not a little unusual for a trainee to travel to interview new clients?"

"The senior partner thinks very well of him," explained Rosie. "One day he will be a partner himself and then we shall be married."

Jack helped himself to more bread. "And will that take long?" he asked carefully.

Rosie turned the dulled ring on her finger and frowned. She often wondered the same thing. "It will take as long as it takes," she retorted loyally. "Arthur is worth waiting for. He says that everything must be right. And when the time is right, he will buy a red brick house with three storeys, a bay window and a garden. I will wear silk instead of calico and I will mix with society."

Jack paused eating for a moment and gave her a studied look. "And what does he do for you in the here and now?"

Rosie pursed her lips together. Surely Jack didn't know her well enough to ask such direct questions, but she found herself bound to answer. "He brings me flowers," she said, and her eyes travelled to the vase of flowers in the middle of the table. The flowers had stood there for a week since Arthur's last visit and were beginning to wilt.

"A strange gift," said Jack, "for a girl who sells flowers for a living."

"Not at all," said Rosie. "Flowers aren't merely flowers you know."

"No?"

"No of course not. Every flower speaks. When folk buy my flowers it's because they have something to say that they cannot put into words for themselves. When I sell periwinkle, I sell 'I hope we can be friends.' When I sell bouquets of hollyhocks and heather, what I'm really selling is 'best of luck'. When I sell forget-me-nots, what I'm really selling is 'Missing you'. Flowers are a language."

Jack leaned across the table. The candlelight illuminated his dark eyes and cast shadows across his chiselled features. "And what do Arthur's flowers say?" he asked.

Rosie took one of the wilting irises from the arrangement. "Arthur always brings me irises," she said. "She ran her fingers along the strong stem. "The stem is long and strong," she said. "It speaks of a 'forever relationship'. The purple petals are gentle, and they talk of truthfulness, honesty and transparency."

A heavy silence hung between them for a moment.

"Would you not prefer roses?" asked Jack looking suddenly unsettled.

"What!" laughed Rosie. "Roses with their 'I love you' message." She cocked her head at him. "Not many men understand the true meaning of love," she said, as though her tender nineteen years qualified her to comment on male sensitivities. "For the time being, I prefer truth."

Jack's face clouded. He got up suddenly and collected together the plates. "The hour is late," he said. He took the plates through to the scullery. "The meal was delicious," he said. "Yet again I am in your debt."

Rosie studied the stem of iris in her hand and knew a sudden moment of conscience. She took the candle and followed Jack into the kitchen. She watched him washing the dinner plates. She observed that he did not do it well. He was clearly not a man used to domesticity. "Jack," she said. "I have to confess that I haven't been entirely truthful," she said.

He cast a questioning look.

"The house does not belong to me," she said.

"Who then?"

She shrugged. "Nobody!" she set the candle down and sat on the scullery stool. "My father died when I was fifteen years old and I was left with nothing and nowhere to live. To begin with I slept in a doorway opposite this dairy. The old man who lived in the dairy had a horse and a cart. He delivered milk every morning in the early hours. Then one day the horse grew old and died. The old man took to pushing the cart, but I noticed that given his age, he could not push the cart very easily. Well I'm resourceful me you see, and I spotted an opportunity. I told him I would push the cart for him in return for a bed in his horse's stable loft. He had no use for the stable nor the loft now that his horse was dead."

"The same stable loft you have offered me?" asked Jack.

Rosie nodded. "Then the old man died too. I was the only person who went to his funeral. There were no other mourners. He had no family."

"So you moved into the old man's house," said Jack guessing the rest of her story.

Rosie nodded. "Was that so wrong?" she asked. "The old man had left money in a tin on the kitchen shelf," she went on. "Well the dead have no use for money, do they? So I spent it on flowers I knew would sell, cleaned up the old milk cart and set up in business. Who could blame me for that? Not dishonest. Just resourceful. That's all."

"But Rosie," said Jack softly. "You must know that someone somewhere must own the house. The old man must have had some descendants, and one day they will come. In the meantime, it's probably best that you don't speak of this to anyone."

"I only speak of it to you," said Rosie, "because I think it's best to be truthful, don't you?"

Jack cast her an uneasy look and said nothing.

"I know perfectly well that one day someone will come and take the house from me," said Rosie. "But I've got to live somewhere, and the stable loft was cold in winter, and the doorway was even colder. I'm just making the best of the house whilst it's empty. You see I'm..."

"...Resourceful!" finished Jack with a grin.

Chapter Two

Arthur Tipple came strutting through the crowds. He was small for a man, just five foot six, but he held his head high and gave the impression of someone much taller. His brown hair was worn slightly longer than was fashionable and was combed impeccably under a bowler hat perched at a slightly jaunty angle. He wore a well-tailored navy suit with a square of silk in the top pocket and a gold watch chain draped across his waistcoat.

He stopped in his tracks for a moment. He thought for a moment he'd heard a nightingale! To hear a nightingale on a mid-winter morning in London was unlikely. He looked round and spotted Sparrow. Sparrow's mouth was puckered up in one of his famous bird calls. The market goers automatically stopped to hear Sparrow do his impressions of lark a song thrush or a chaffinch and once they had stopped, they would more than likely buy one of Sparrow's finches or at the very least, a cone of chestnuts, pastries, fresh eels or flowers.

Arthur Tipple grinned good naturedly and pretended to box Sparrow's ears. "You got me then," he said. "Good and proper."

"Where were you when we needed you then?" asked Sparrow cheekily.

"Important work," said Arthur adjusting his cravat nervously. "Couldn't be helped. Where's our Rosie?"

"Not that we needed you," said Sparrow. "This new bloke turned up. You should have seen him fight off the Heneghans. He fought like ten men."

"Fifteen more like," said Will from behind the pastry barrow.

"Twenty even!" said Charlie.

Arthur's cocksure grin dropped a little. He helped himself to a pastry and tossed a ha'penny in Charlie's direction. "So who is he then?" asked Arthur. "This bloke who fights like twenty men."

"His name's Jack," said Will.

"And he's moved in with your Rosie," said Charlie maliciously.

Arthur paused with the pastry suspended halfway into his mouth. He looked round and spotted Rosie's barrow. Rosie was busy selling lilies to an old lady who was on her way to a funeral. Arthur strode over his face grim. He got hold of Rosie's arm. "'Ere," he said. "A word." He steered her away to a quieter spot. "What's this I hear about you moving in with some upstart?"

Rosie felt a jolt of indignation followed by a flutter of gratification. That Arthur cared for her enough to feel jealousy was surely a good sign. For a moment she wanted to fuel the jealousy, but she knew better than that. "Arthur Tipple," she said instead. "Are you insinuating that I would move in with a man I had known for less than an hour?"

"Well..." faltered Arthur losing ground.

"A man we've never seen before came to our rescue yesterday," explained Rosie. "And who could blame us for the gratitude we felt at being rescued from the Heneghans, especially as you didn't turn up as promised."

Arthur flinched.

"Then because the man was all dressed in rags and with nowhere to lay his head," went on Rosie enjoying Arthur's discomfit, "I offered him the loft over the stable."

Arthur sagged with relief. "So you have not moved in with him?"

"Of course not," said Rosie. "Arthur Tipple what do you take me for? How could you even suggest it?"

Arthur wound his arms around her possessively. "I'm sorry to have doubted you," he said. "It's just that I love you so much and you're so very beautiful." He twisted a tendril of her long red hair around his fingers. "I can't help but worry every day that someone will come along and sweep you off your feet." He slid his arms around her waist and pulled her close. She looked up into his chestnut brown eyes. For the millionth time she marvelled at how disarming his boyish grin was. When she saw the dimples play mischievously around the edges of his mouth, she could forgive him anything.

"Well perhaps you should hurry up and marry me then," grinned Rosie.

"Did you save last night's tea for me?" asked Arthur presumptuously. "I could call on you this evening."

"But it's Saturday!" said Rosie surprised. "You never call on a Saturday. Friday is 'Arthur's Day'."

"Well from now on," said Arthur, "any day of the week when I am not called upon to travel is 'Arthur's Day'."

Rosie threw her arms around Arthur's and reached up for a kiss. "I love you so much Arthur Tipple," she said. "Do we really need to wait for you to finish your accountancy training before we can marry?"

Arthur took Rosie's face in his hands and kissed her very tenderly. "Yes, I think we must wait," he said. "I want everything to be right for my Rosie. Once I am a partner, I will buy you a proper diamond ring. We will have the finest of weddings." He kissed her again. "And we shall have a big well-to-do house with bay windows, sunny rooms and a roof that doesn't leak."

Rosie closed her eyes the better to enjoy Arthur's kisses and the better to enjoy the fantasy. She couldn't wait to be Mrs Tipple.

Jack tapped on the scullery door. "I've got you a gift," he told Rosie. "Just something to show a mark of my appreciation. Come and look."

Rosie looked up at him quizzically. Then she fetched an oil lamp and followed him out into the darkness of the back yard. In a corner where until now there had been nothing but weeds, was a large wooden box with a double lid that opened upwards.

"It's a coal bunker," explained Jack.

Rosie laughed. "I've always wanted a coal bunker," she confessed. "What a pity it isn't full of coal."

"But it is." Jack opened the lid to reveal that the bunker was filled to the rim with lumps of glistening coal.

Rosie's eyes shot wide with astonishment. "How did you get it?"

"Don't ask!" grinned Jack. "I'm resourceful me."

Rosie placed her hands on her hips. "As long as you didn't do anything that will bring the police knocking," she said. "I'll go and fetch the scuttle and make up a fire. It's a good night for a fire. Arthur will be calling shortly."

"On a Saturday?" said Jack raising his eyebrows. "I thought Friday was 'Arthur's night'."

Uncharacteristically punctual, Arthur knocked at seven on the dot just as he had promised. He was bearing a gift of fifteen red roses.

"Arthur Tipple!" gasped Rosie. "How much brass have you just put in another flower seller's pocket?"

Arthur dropped a kiss onto the end of her nose. "That's not the point as well you know," he said.

So what was the point? Rosie took the roses and breathed in their heady scent. The roses should say, "I love you." Instead, their message seemed to speak more of Arthur's insecurity that the man living outside in the stable loft might steal Rosie from him.

Arthur stepped into the kitchen and warmed his hands at the roaring fire. It was unusual to see such a good fire in Rosie's kitchen and he stayed there a while with his fingers splayed over the dancing flames. He sniffed the oxtail broth and observed the candle lit table with its mis-matched china with a faint smile. He knew it was all for him. He sat at the table and breathed easy. Nothing had changed. Rosie loved him as much as she had always done.

Rosie dished up two bowls of oxtail broth. There wasn't quite as much oxtail in the broth as there had been the day before. Rosie did her best to dish the lion's share of the meat into Arthur's dish.

"This is delicious," remarked Arthur. "Though when we are married we shall eat steak, and we will have china that matches." He noted the dreamy look in Rosie's eyes and warmed to his subject. "And we shall have cut glass champagne flutes with which to celebrate the arrival of our first child."

Rosie looked up at him sharply. "Where were you yesterday when we needed you?" she asked suddenly.

Arthur slid his hands across the table and took her fingers in his. "If only I could have got a message to you," he said. "The senior partner asked me to pay a visit to a very important prospective client in Harrow."

"More important than your fiancée?" asked Rosie pointedly.

"There was a very healthy commission involved," went on Arthur. "The company trades in gemstones from India." His tone became suddenly admonishing. "Enrolling companies like this onto the books of Leadbetter and Weightman will get us the commissions that will pay for our wedding and house."

There was a gentle tap on the scullery door and Jack popped his head round the kitchen door. "I'm sorry to interrupt," he said sounding not one bit sorry. "May I take a wash at the scullery sink?"

"Is here no pump in the back yard?" asked Arthur with a ferocious glare.

Jack appeared not to notice the ferocious glare and moved across the small room to shake Arthur Tipple's hand. "Mr Tipple I presume," he said. "I've heard a lot about you."

Arthur was left with no option but to shake Jack's hand. "You have baby soft hands for someone supposed to do manual work for a living," commented Arthur bitchily.

"And you have very course hands," returned Jack swiftly, "for a clerk!"

"Trainee accountant," corrected Arthur narrowing his eyes.

"I shall pour some tea," said Rosie disappointed that the men had not got off to a better start. She fetched an extra cup and poured tea for three.

"It is good to meet you," said Jack studying Arthur Tipple from over the top of his teacup. "It would have been even better to have met you yesterday."

Rosie frowned. What right did Jack have to scold her fiancé? "It's not up to you to point a finger," she said sternly. She turned to Arthur. "Tell him," she said. "Tell Jack why you were not able to be here yesterday."

Arthur seemed suddenly unwilling to explain himself. "I don't have to justify myself to your 'lodger'," he said curtly.

But for some reason Rosie felt oddly compelled to explain her fiancé's absence. "An important job, that's why not," said Rosie. "Tell him Arthur." But again, Arthur shook his head with a frown. "Arthur will be a partner one day at Leadbetter and Weightman," went on Rosie proudly. "And part of his training is to go and interview new clients. Isn't that right Arthur? Yesterday Arthur had to see a firm in Harrow whose business it is buy precious gemstones from India. It was obviously very important for Leadbetter and Weightman to secure this very important business."

She poured more tea and squeezed more lemon. Surely now that Jack understood Arthur a little better, they should all get along more amicably.

Jack gave Arthur Tipple a very hard stare. "I'm surprised given at how very important the business was, that a senior partner would trust a clerk with the visit."

"Trainee accountant," corrected Arthur for the second time, and the veins in the side of his head were beginning to pulsate.

Jack stirred his tea thoughtfully. "I happen to know Harrow quite well," he said. "I might know the firm you went to visit. May I ask the name of it?"

"No, you may not ask the name of it," snapped Arthur. "It's confidential."

"Yes it would be," murmured Jack.

Arthur leapt to his feet knocking his chair over. "Why don't you come straight out with it and call me a liar?" he ground out.

"Oh Arthur!" Rosie pulled at his sleeve in an effort to calm him down. "No one is calling you a liar."

"He is!" said Arthur. "You're not hearing him. He's calling me a liar." He rounded on Jack. "At least I have a job. At least I'm not a ne'er-do-well beggar presuming on the good will of a young girl." He took off his jacket and poised his fists in a boxing attitude. "For two pins I'll give you a good pummelling for your trouble."

Jack took a long slow sip of tea. "If you are looking for a fight Mr Tipple I will give you a fight. But I have to warn you that I will win." He rose lazily to his feet and his height filled the room.

Arthur regarded Jack's height and bulk at proximity, and he swallowed hard.

"Enough!" cried Rosie and she placed herself between the two sparring men. "What way is this for two grown men to behave? How dare you propose a fight under my roof. Both of you should leave right now." She turned to Jack. "I shall bid you a good night."

Jack looked suddenly contrite.

"And you!" Rosie turned on Arthur. "I would have expected better of you Arthur Tipple."

Arthur snatched up his coat. "Not my place to say that you can or cannot take a lodger in your stable loft," he said. "But when we have our own house, I shall absolutely forbid it." And with that he stalked off into the night.

Jack washed the dishes at the scullery sink. "I'm sorry that I spoilt your evening Rosie," he said looking genuinely remorseful. "There is just something about Mr Tipple that I do not trust."

"That you either trust or mistrust my fiancé is none of your concern," said Rosie. She took the wilting irises from their vase and crushed them into the bin. She replaced them with the fifteen red roses. The roses did not fill the vase as vibrantly as the iris had done, and for some reason that she couldn't fathom, they didn't fill her with the same joy.

"Think Eddie has sold more eels in one week than he's sold all year since Jack arrived," commented Ma' Maggie tossing chestnuts onto a hot griddle.

Rosie looked across the barrows curiously. Jack seemed to have taken young Eddie under his wing. Eddie's palsy had left him unable to speak and so Jack had become his voice.

"Fresh eels ladies and gents!" shouted Jack and his rich clear voice travelled easily across the market. "First catch of the day."

Ma' Maggie cackled. "He's good him!"

A few passers-by stopped to look into the eel trays.

"Meal fit for a king," prompted Jack. "And just for a penny or two."

Rosie smiled faintly. She hadn't quite forgiven him for his obvious contempt for Arthur.

"Fry 'em up with a bit of butter," went on Jack helping Eddie with the speed of sales by wrapping eels in newspaper. "Stew 'em in a savoury sauce."

"Don't know where he came from," said Ma' Maggie, "but he's making such a difference."

Rosie sat behind her barrow tying little bouquets of carnations with pink ribbon and lace. It was true. Since Jack had arrived, life had suddenly become a lot easier. He might not have any money to pay rent for the stable loft, but he had kept the bunker full of coal by means he had kept secret, and he had been doing lots of odd jobs around the house and yard. He cleaned out the fire every morning fishing out the little lumps of unburned coal and emptying the ash. She had come home one night to find a broken windowpane mended which she had long been trying to shield from the whistling drafts, and to her delight some of the leaking roof tiles had been mysteriously patched too. Then every so often he would come home with generous cuts of expensive beef the likes of which she could never have afforded on her meagre flower money.

It wasn't just Rosie's life that had improved since Jack's arrival. Jack was surprisingly good at whipping up trade for the little group of barrow traders. He had taken to mingling and chatting to ladies and gentlemen at the richer end of the market suggesting better value from the barrow vendors. Despite his ragged appearance, Jack had an easy charm and a presence that won people's immediate liking. Before they knew it, Rosie and her little adopted family were doubling their business and could hardly keep up.

Ma' Maggie hoisted a pile of old newspapers onto her barrow. "Look at what Jack got us," she cackled. "Old newspaper to wrap the flowers and the eels and to make cones for the hot chestnuts." She spread the newspapers and smoothed them flat with her hands. "And not just any local rag neither," she said. "The Times no less. Jack says to me, 'Don't ask how I got them', and taps the side of his nose." She cackled again.

On the top sheet something caught Rosie's eye. She picked up the sheet and her hands trembled slightly. She felt the blood draining from her face. From amongst the advertisements for the latest elixirs and steamship travel, an advertisement jumped out at her.

"What's the matter ducks," asked Ma' Maggie noting Rosie's suddenly ashen face.

"This!" Rosie showed Ma' Maggie the paper. Ma' Maggie looked at it blankly. She had never learned to read. Rosie, who had learned to read a little at Sunday School, slowly read the advertisement aloud, guessing at some of the longer words. "Finest office supplies provided by Arthur Tipple," she read. "For the discerning gentleman or lady of business seeking highest quality office essentials. Look no further than Arthur Tipple, your trusted purveyor of fine office supplies. An exquisite range of products to elevate your business affairs. Impeccable ledgers, quills of elegance, inks of distinction delivered to your door. Enquire by letter in the first instance to Mr Arthur Tipple esquire at 21 Fotheringhay Road Kensington."

"Arthur Tipple," said Ma Maggie slowly. "Not your Arthur Tipple surely. Your Arthur Tipple is a trainee accountant, not a travelling salesman selling quills and inks."

"No," said Rosie. "It can't be the same Arthur Tipple. Most likely there are lots of Arthur Tipples in London."

"Most likely," said Ma' Maggie.

"My Arthur Tipple would not have told me such dreadful lies," said Rosie loyally.

"Of course not," said Ma' Maggie.

A silence hung between them. There was a terrible doubt creeping into Rosie's mind. She remembered when she had sent Sparrow to run and fetch Arthur the day the Heneghans had attacked only to be told that it 'wasn't Arthur's day'. Might Arthur only visit Leadbetter and Weightman's on certain days to sell stationery supplies?

"Funny ain't it," said Ma' Maggie slyly, "that the advertisement happened to be on the top sheet!"

Rosie looked over quickly at Jack who was still helping Eddie to sell his eels. Could Jack have already known about the advertisement and placed it strategically so that Rosie would see it too? Jack glanced over in her direction and noticed that she was staring. He gave her a smile and a little wave. He didn't look like a man with a bad conscience.

"I shall put this out of my mind," said Rosie firmly. "The Arthur Tipple in the advertisement is clearly not my Arthur Tipple."

"Clearly not," said Ma' Maggie. "But if you wanted to know for sure, you could pay number twenty-one Fotheringhay Avenue a little visit."

Rosie shook her head firmly. "That would be a dreadful betrayal of trust," she said. "I would never do that!"

Chapter Three

A thick fog was settling over 21 Fotheringhay Road. Each window glowed with a smudge of candlelight. Rosie pulled her shawl tightly around her shoulders and walked purposefully along the row of well-appointed town houses each with its own scrubbed step, bay window and polished knocker. Arthur had often described how he lived with his mother in a small two bedroomed house. His mother wasn't of sound mind, he had told her, and this was the reason Rosie could not visit. His mother, he had explained, harboured a terror of being taken to live in the asylum and could not tolerate strangers calling. Rosie stopped at number 21. This house did not look anything like the house Arthur had described he and his mother sharing. All the same, Rosie had to be certain. She stepped boldly up to the door and rapped the knocker. The knocker seemed to upset the people who lived inside. A baby started to wail. Another child began to shout. Then came a woman's voice flustered and chiding. There came the sound of shuffling feet and the door swung open. Rosie saw a woman not much older than herself well-dressed but wearing an apron and a harassed expression. She carried a baby on one hip. Another child peered up at Rosie from behind his mother's skirts. From somewhere in the house another child was howling. It felt to Rosie as though the whole house must be filled with children. She knew a wave of relief. The Arthur Tipple who lived here was clearly not her Arthur Tipple. The Arthur Tipple who lived here clearly had a wife and children. This Arthur Tipple clearly did not live alone with an ageing mother.

"Yes?" challenged the woman on the doorstep.

"Is this the residence of Mr Arthur Tipple?" asked Rosie, then noting the other woman's suspicious glance, fished the newspaper advertisement from her pocket. "I've come to enquire after some of Mr Tipple's office services."

The other woman afforded a brief smile. "It's more usual for prospective customers to write in the first instance," she said, "but I'll see if he will make time for you."

Rosie stood waiting. Nerves began to flutter in her stomach. This Arthur Tipple would not be her Arthur Tipple she kept telling herself. A moment later she heard light footsteps coming down the staircase. She saw a dapper man with brown well combed hair. She saw a man in a smart suit with a gold chain draped across the waistcoat pocket. It was Arthur. It was Rosie's Arthur. Rosie felt a rush of shock. Her senses reeled. Her normally strong grip on reality swam. Arthur stopped dead in his tracks and his usual easy smile froze. He was just as shocked to see Rosie as she was to see him.

"Don't be too long Arthur," said the other woman planting a kiss on the end of her husband's nose. "I am about to serve the tea." She hurried off with the children in tow.

Arthur grabbed his jacket from the end of the bannister rail and stepped out of the house. He took hold of Rosie's arm non too gently and steered her away from the house.

"Rosie! What do you think you are doing here?" His face was twisted in sudden anger as though she had broken some unspoken rule.

"Take your hand off me!" ground out Rosie.

He let go of her and confusion overtook his initial anger. Rosie pulled the advertisement from her pocket and waved it at him accusingly. "Ma' Maggie and I spotted it," she said. "I refused to believe it was you. I stood up for you." Her lip began to tremble. "I said that the Arthur Tipple in the advertisement could not be the man who had promised to marry me.

The Arthur Tipple, who was a travelling salesman, could not be the same Arthur Tipple who had been promised a partnership at Leadbetter and Weightman's. The Arthur Tipple who had asked me to be his wife..." she began to sob, "could not be married already with children."

"Rosie please don't cry." Arthur went to take her in his arms.

Rosie jumped back as though she had been stung. Disappointment and fury gave her the strength to recover her tears. "You have lied and deceived me, and you have lied and deceived your wife. You are despicable."

"I ask only that you don't tell my wife of this," said Arthur and his eyes darted to and fro nervously.

Rosie gave him a long look. He seemed to have shrunk in stature. He suddenly resembled a hunted animal. "No words of regret," she said softly. "No words of love. No plea for forgiveness. Just a request to help cover your tracks."

She took off the little brass engagement ring and passed it back to him. Then she pulled herself up to her full height and stuck her chin in the air. "Don't worry," she said with a scornful look. "I will not give away your indiscretion to your wife. It's up to you to put your house in order."

Arthur sagged with relief and regained a little of his former cocksure self. "And perhaps," he said carefully, "we might still see each other. After all, is it not possible to love two people?"

It was hard to know that the very high regard in which Rosie had held Arthur only the day before could have fallen so far and so fast. "Do not attempt to call on me again," she said. "I will see you again, but only on Judgement Day." And with that, Rosie turned and walked away without looking back. She was conscious that Arthur was standing looking after her, but she resisted the temptation to take one last look.

As Rosie walked into the thickening fog, she felt herself trembling from head to foot. Her jaw, that had begun to ache with the effort of holding back tears suddenly gave way to a tide of uncontrollable sobs. She could scarcely believe it. The future she had dreamt of and placed her belief in for so long was over. She was grateful that the fog that had descended so quickly disguised her tear-streaked face from passers-by. She kept her head down anxious to get home without being seen; anxious to shut her own front door on her misery.

The Bow Bells were striking three by the time Rosie reached the top of her street. Despite the early hour the daylight had already ebbed. It was the sort of day that couldn't be bothered to grow light before it was growing dark again. Already the lamp lighter was lighting the streetlamps illuminating little halos of blurred white and yellow against the fog. Rosie stopped dead in her tracks. In the eerie glow of the gas light, she saw a man and a woman outside her house peering through the front window. The man was tall with raven-like features, a top hat and a billowing woollen overcoat. The woman was petite, her slim figure hidden beneath layers of satin and lace. Dark curls spilled around her face from beneath an elegant bonnet. Rosie stepped back into the shadows. The couple were clearly not neighbours. The couple were clearly not from this end of London. Rosie was overtaken by a deep sense of foreboding. It was never far from her mind that one day someone could come and reclaim the house. Could this couple be descendants of the old man whose house she had adopted as her own?

Rosie stepped back into the shadows. Perhaps if she waited long enough, the couple would go away again. It wasn't to be. At that precise moment Jack stepped out of the tavern on the corner and sauntered back towards the stable loft he called home with his chin buried in his scarf against the fog. He stopped outside Rosie's home. The lamp light illuminated his broad shoulders and the pale features of the young woman who was questioning him and pointing towards the house. She was looking increasingly irate, and Jack was gesturing appeasement. He was clearly trying to diffuse the situation. Rosie sighed. She knew a moment of dread. Could this day get any worse? One thing was for certain, she couldn't stay hidden in the shadows. She picked up the hem of her skirt and hurried down the street. Jack spotted her emerging from the fog and reached out a reassuring arm. Rosie side stepped his over familiarity and addressed the couple directly.

"Can I help you?" she asked.

"Rosie," said Jack gently. "This young woman is Maryanne Hadley. She is the niece of Tom Hadley, the old man who owned this house. She has come to view her inheritance and is... er... surprised to find someone living here."

Rosie had practised this moment lots of times in her head, but now she was at a loss. "Let us discuss this indoors," she said, and her hand shook slightly as she put the key in the lock and let the couple into her small kitchen. Rosie frowned slightly to find Jack stepping uninvited into the kitchen alongside her. Surely this was none of his business, yet she felt strangely reassured. She had lived this moment so many times. In her imagination it had always been Arthur at her side.

Maryanne Hadley surveyed her inheritance in ill-disguised disdain. Her eye rested on the damp stains and the peeling plaster and she took a small lavender doused handkerchief from her pocket and held it to her dainty retroussé nose.

Rosie threw some kindling on the fire and hung the kettle over the flames. "Would anyone care for tea?" she asked.

Maryanne glanced at the old china cups in horror and shook her head.

"May I?" said the tall man with hawk features requesting permission to spread his paperwork on the table and get on with the business in hand.

The four sat down at the table and the man spread out the paperwork by the candlelight.

"I am Henry Blunt," said the man. "I am Miss Hadley's solicitor and the executor of Tom Hadley's estate." He looked quizzically over the top of his spectacles at Rosie and Jack. "Forgive me," he said. "We were totally unaware that Tom Hadley had tenants."

Rosie opened her mouth to speak but Jack spoke first.

"Yes we are tenants," said Jack not entirely untruthfully. He turned to Maryanne and switched on his most charming smile. "I hope Miss Hadley, that you are able to continue the arrangement your uncle put in place. We are of course willing to re-negotiate the terms."

Maryanne Hadley was not won over by Jack's charming smile. She pursed up her lips and sent her solicitor a quick frown.

"My client and I have already discussed this," said Henry Blunt carefully. "Miss Hadley has no interest in keeping the property as a business proposition. She is keen to sell the house as quickly as possible."

Rosie regarded Maryanne Hadley with dislike. She wondered if the other woman in her fine satin and lace had ever known a day's hardship. She noted the other woman's spoilt mouth and vacant eyes and knew that Jack would not appeal to finer feelings in a woman who clearly did not have any finer feelings.

"I'm sorry," said Mr Blunt looking to Jack rather than Rosie, "but unless you have evidence of a written contractual agreement?"

Rosie shook her head unhappily.

"Then I must ask you to move out at your earliest convenience," finished Mr Blunt.

"By the end of the week," put in Maryanne Hadley sharply. "I already have a buyer in mind."

"I'm sorry," said Mr Blunt again looking genuinely sympathetic and his client shot him a look of irritation.

Jack pulled himself to his feet. "Well if that's all," he said. "I'll walk with you to the market square and hail you a carriage. It can be difficult at this hour."

"That's very kind of you," said Mr Blunt. He tipped his hat in Rosie's direction. "Good evening Miss."

Rosie stood at the door and watched Jack walk their two visitors away. She wondered why he was bothering to help them find a cab. She went back into the house struggling to collect her thoughts. She had lost her fiancé and her house in the same day. The future suddenly looked very bleak indeed. The roses that Arthur had given her only days earlier were still opening up their faces to the world. Rosie scowled down at them. They spoke the same lies Arthur had spoken. They spoke of undying love and fidelity. She took them from their vase and buried her nose in the petals trying to discern their scent. All she could smell was the smoke from the fire that had given up struggling its way up a wet chimney and was billowing back into the kitchen.

Rosie crushed the roses fiercely into the bin. The thorns scratched her hands and drew blood. She leaned her forehead against the scullery window and gave way to tears all over again. She cried long and hard wondering how there could be any tears left to cry.

From behind her came the quiet click of a door. It was Jack. He tactfully pretended not to see her hastily wiping her eyes.

"Things are not as bad as you might think," he said.

"How so?" scowled Rosie. "We have no home. You heard what Miss Hadley said. We have to move out as soon as possible. We are back on the streets."

"Well I'm not going anywhere," said Jack with a slight smile. "Neither are you. I've sorted it all out. This is still your home, and the stable loft is still mine."

"How?" Rosie scrunched up her face in puzzlement.

"You don't need to know how," he said. "But Miss Hadley and Mr Blunt will not be back. Trust me."

The memory of how Jack had single handedly fought off the Heneghan brothers with his bare fists came back to her. A strange sensation twisted in her gut.

"What have you done?" she asked fearfully.

"You don't need to know," he repeated. He took her hands and noticed that they were beaded in blood. Then he noticed the roses crushed in the bin. "Were they dead?" he asked.

Rosie shook her head numbly. "I no longer plan to marry Mr Tipple," she said.

A silence hung between them for a few seconds.

"I'm genuinely sorry," said Jack putting a protective arm around her. "I had never any liking for Mr Tipple, but I hoped he would make you happy."

For a moment Rosie had the irrational desire to cry on his shoulder. Instead, she snatched up the empty vase from the draining board and rinsed the petals that still clung to the glass.

"It's as I've always maintained," said Rosie fiercely. "Men do not understand the true meaning of love."

Chapter Four

"We've got a present for you," said Will presenting Rosie with a paper bag.

"It's a sugar glazed pastry," said Charlie.

"With spiced fruit," added Will.

"We heard about Arthur," said Charlie as though the gift needed an explanation.

"I always thought he was a wrong 'un," said Will loyally.

Rosie bent to reach the two boys and scooped them up in a big hug. "Thank you," she said. "What would I do without you?"

"I'd give you one of my finches," said Sparrow magnanimously, "but they take a lot of looking after."

Rosie gave a choked sort of laugh. "Thank you Sparrow," she said giving him a friendly cuff. "Thank you boys. You're more family to me than any real family could be." Then she stopped in her tracks and looked to where Eddie usually set up his barrow.

"Where's Eddie this morning?" she asked with a sudden frown."

"Did Jack not mention it?" said Ma' Maggie. "He's taken Eddie to see some doctor. Not any old doctor. A special doctor. A doctor what fixes twisted arms and legs."

"But that would cost lots of money," said Rosie mystified. "However would Jack afford that?"

"Well you know Jack," cackled Ma' Maggie. "He managed to get if for free. Better still, the doctor is going to pay Ed's grandfather so he can research the boy's condition."

"Research!" echoed Rosie horrified. "What does that mean? I'll tell you what that means. They'll prod him with needles and experiment with potions. I won't have it. I won't have Eddie treated like that."

"Of course not," said Ma' Maggie quietly. "We all want the best for the boy and Jack won't let the doctor experiment with needles and the like. You want to see Eddie get well don't you?"

Rosie bit her lip. She was angry with Jack. Helping Eddie sell his eels was one thing but taking him off to see some 'quack' most likely without the full understanding of the grandfather who cared for him was quite another.

"And that's not all," piped up Will oblivious to Rosie's mounting consternation. "Jack said he's found a school that will take me and Charlie and Sparrow. We're going to learn to read and write."

Rosie spun round on Ma' Maggie. "What's going on here?" she demanded.

Ma' Maggie shrugged. "It's good ain't it?" she asked.

Rosie turned to the twins. "You don't need school," she persisted. "Selling pastries is what you do best. You'll never be out of work. Folks will always want pastries. And what can school teach you about breeding birds?" she asked Sparrow. "Why didn't you ask me if an education was what you wanted. I can teach you to read and write."

The boys shifted uncomfortably.

"But Rosie," said Sparrow. "Jack said school will make gentleman of us."

Rosie felt a sudden lump in her throat, and she turned her back hurriedly to hide tears. She felt as though she hated Jack right now. He was breaking up her little adopted family. Who did he think he was?

"I'll never see you again," she sniffed.

Will tugged at her sleeve. "Course you will," he said. "We'll come and see you. We'll come and see you often."

Rosie blinked back the tears. They were deserting her, and worse, they were pitying her. She couldn't bear their pity. She managed a watery grin. "Once you're at school you will make lots of new friends," she said. "You won't want to come back to the market. Ma' Maggie and I wouldn't expect you to."

"No," said Ma' Maggie. "We wouldn't expect you to."

Rosie decided to pack her barrow up early. She was swamped in misery. The loss of Arthur and the news that her little adopted family was going their different ways deepened all around her like a deep abyss. She had always been motivated in selling her flowers knowing that she was saving up for a better life. But now here dreams were in tatters, and nothing seemed worth doing. She pushed her barrow home wearily.

On the way she heard a newspaper seller on the corner hollering the more sensational headlines in an effort to sell newspapers. Rosie stopped for a moment and listened. She was still uncomfortable as to how Jack had dealt with Mr Blunt and Miss Hadley. She half wondered if she might learn that their bodies would be found floating in the Thames. Of course, there was no such news. She pushed her barrow on with a heavy heart and a deep frown. It didn't help that Jack told her so little. It only led her to believe the wildest stories.

Parked outside Rosie's house was a window cleaner's cart. It had the lettering 'Wendell and Son' painted down one side. An old man sat on Rosie's step smoking a pipe. This was clearly Mr Wendell. A young boy teetered on the top of a ladder vigorously cleaning Rosie's windows. This was Mr Wendell's son. Rosie gaped at them in astonishment.

"I think there's been some mistake here," said Rosie to the old man. "I didn't ask for a window cleaner."

"No mistake miss," said Mr Wendell sucking long and hard on his pipe. "We clean these every Wednesday."

"But I can't afford a window cleaner!" said Rosie weakly.

"Well you don't need to bother your pretty young head with that," said the old man. "Your hubby has been taking care of it."

"Hubby?" repeated Rosie blankly.

"Yes, him in there!" Mr Wendell gestured towards the house with his head.

Yet again Rosie's stomach knotted. She had only known Jack for a matter of weeks, but in that very short space of time he had managed to take over every corner of her life. Since that fateful day Jack had burst onto the scene and beaten off the Heneghan brothers, nothing had stayed the same, and she didn't like it.

Rosie parked her barrow. She stepped around Mr Wendell and into the house. She found Jack on his knees cleaning the kitchen grate and laying fresh kindling and coal. He looked up quickly as her shadow fell across the kitchen.

"You're home early," said Jack, and his tone belied that he was feeling 'caught out'.

She regarded him coolly. "Do you think it was your place to employ the services of a window cleaner?" she asked.

"You like clean windows don't you?" he asked evasively. "You've been commenting on how much brighter the rooms look."

"I liked clean windows when I thought it was you who was cleaning them," said Rosie.

"What's the difference?" shrugged Jack. He attempted a disarming smile, but it died on his lips.

"The truth," said Rosie. "That's the difference."

"I never said that it was me who was cleaning the windows," said Jack not meeting her eye.

"Where did you get the money?" asked Rosie. "I can only think that you have stolen it."

Anger flashed across Jack's face at being accused of theft. "You don't need to know where I got the money," he said.

"Stop saying that I don't need to know," said Rosie beginning to lose her temper. "I *do* need to know. I need to know who you are. I need to know where you came from. I need to know how you get the coal and the best joints of beef. I need to know how you got a doctor for Eddie and a school for Will, Charlie and Sparrow. I need to know how you saw off Miss Hadley and her solicitor. I need answers."

Jack studied her for a long moment. "Is it not enough to know that I have changed everything for the better?" he asked.

"No, it's not enough!" snapped Rosie. "And you haven't changed everything for the better. You've changed everything for the worse. Everything was fine the way it was. This time last month I was happy." Rosie's voice began to tremble. "Now I have nothing."

"Happy?" Jack's eyebrows shot up into his hairline. "Happy with a fiancé who was cheating and lying? Happy waiting for the owner of your home to come along and evict you?"

"Who do you think you are?" Rosie began to pace. "The boys don't need a school. How will their mother make money now from all her baking? And Eddie! Does the boy's grandfather understand that this doctor you have found will be prodding him with needles and practising all sorts of quack cures?"

"So what is this really about?" asked Jack carefully.

Rosie struggled against tears. "They were like family to me," she managed. "They were my only family. You've spoilt everything. Now I have no one."

"Rosie," said Jack gently. "The boys want to go to school. I found a shop that will buy their mother's pastries for double what the boys were selling them for on the barrows. You want the boys to do well don't you? Do you not want them to grow up with choices?"

Rosie wiped her nose roughly on her sleeve. She knew that she mustn't stand in the boys' way.

"And as for Ed's grandfather," went on Jack. "He is growing too old and too ill to care for the boy. He's only too happy for his grandson to stay with the doctor and his wife for a while. You want Eddie to be well don't you? This doctor is bound to improve his condition. He may even find a cure."

Rosie scowled. She didn't want to listen to the voice of reason. "I want my old life back," she said stubbornly. "I have no one now but Ma' Maggie."

Jack got up from cleaning the grate and stepped towards her. With his back to the window he blocked the light. But even in the semi darkness his eyes glittered. "You have me," he said. And he went to take her hands in his.

For one moment Rosie knew a desire to cling to him. She stepped back appalled. It was barely a day since she had lost the love of her life. Why was she even considering falling into another man's arms?

"Why would I want you?" she said her grief making her crueller than she intended. "It is you who has spoilt everything." Her words tumbled out in a tangle of mixed emotion. "Nothing is the same since you arrived. In fact, it would better if you left."

Jack looked as though he had been struck. "Do you really mean that?"

"Yes I do," snapped Rosie. "Go back to wherever you came from. I intend to get my life back and I can only get my life back without you in it."

She turned her back to signal that this was the end of the matter. A silence descended, and when she eventually ventured to turn around, she found herself completely alone.

The next day dawned bleak. The sky was an unforgiving grey, and everything was covered in thick layers of steely frost. Rosie wrapped up in her warmest shawl and fingerless gloves and pushed her barrow to the wholesalers on the way to the market. For the past few weeks Jack had been collecting Rosie's stock from the wholesalers allowing her an extra hour in bed. To have to get up in the dark and call at the wholesalers at dawn was a stark reminder of how hard things had been before.

When Rosie reached the market Ma' Maggie was already there lighting the charcoal under the griddle where she cooked the chestnuts. The old lady was surprised not to see Jack. "What's he up to this morning then?" she asked.

Rosie shrugged. "He's gone," she whispered. "We won't be seeing him again."

A look of consternation spread over the old woman's face. "Gone?" she repeated numbly. "Who's going to keep the Heneghan brothers at bay now? How are we going to get the newspapers he brought for the chestnut cones? I'll be back to begging for them again! And who's going to drive customers our way from the posh end?"

Rosie's heart sank. Had she done something very selfish in telling Jack to go? She hadn't thought how much Ma' Maggie had come to rely upon him. "We will manage every bit as well as we did before," said Rosie arranging bouquets and posies. She glanced over the cobbles at where Eddie and the other boys would normally set up their barrows. Her heart sank further still. She would miss the sudden roars of laughter that the twins were prone to. She would miss Sparrow's clever bird calls and how they brought curious market goers over to their end of the market.

Stuck at the poorer end of the market with only Ma' Maggie for company, Rosie knew it would be harder to whip up trade without Jack's help. Jack she knew would have been using his powerful voice and witty repartee to call over prospective customers. Jack she knew would have been moving around the market, mingling with wealthier customers and directing them over to the barrows for a bargain. Rosie sighed. As the day wore on, she became increasingly aware of how little she had sold. She would certainly not have enough money to buy any meat to go with her evening meal. The sky grew dark and the more well-off stall holders were lighting little paraffin lanterns and hanging them beneath the stall awnings. Rosie had no way to light her barrow and decided to go home. She walked with a deliberate spring in her step tying to keep up her own spirits. A couple of weeks ago she had not needed Jack and she did not need him now. But as she parked her barrow and let herself into her house she was struck by just how dark and cold and empty the house was without him. The ashes lay in the grate from the night before, and there was only one shovel of coal left in the bunker. She decided to riddle the ash rather than clean the grate from scratch. She lit a very frugal fire. Then she cooked a blind broth trying not to worry about tomorrow's tea. After all, she was resourceful. She had managed before, and she would manage again.

Rosie sat as close to the fire as she could and warmed her hands on a bowl of hot pot. She had strict words with herself. "You're only missing Jack for what he could bring," she told herself. "Coal, and lean beef and window cleaners. Those things do not bring happiness." But deep down she knew she was missing more than this. She missed that he cared. She dropped her spoon in sudden realisation. She had spent her whole day missing Jack. Not once had she thought of Arthur Tipple. Could she really be this fickle? Perhaps she had not loved Arthur in the first place.

She helped herself to another bowl of broth knowing that she would regret it the next day when there was nothing left to eat. She tried to work out when she had first nurtured feelings for Jack. Perhaps it was the day he had used an old crate as a springboard to land both his boots into the centre of Morgan Heneghan's chest.

Outside on the street, revellers made their way homewards. Rosie looked at the dying embers. With nothing left to burn, it was time she decided to go up to bed. She was just about to extinguish the candles when there was a gentle tap on the front door. Rosie pulled back the curtain and peeped from the window. She saw a tall man standing at the door and with a rush of emotion she recognised that it was Jack. She knew a sudden urge to run to the door, but she took care to take her time.

Jack stood under the streetlamp. He looked down at her, uncharacteristically nervous. "I have no words," he said. "So I bought you these." He handed her a large bunch of purple hyacinths. Their little bell petals peeped up at her from their newspaper wrapping. Their powerful scent washed over her drowning out the sooty smell of the surrounding chimneys.

"They bring a message," explained Jack. "They're saying..."

"...Forgive me," interrupted Rosie with a smile. "Purple hyacinths say, 'forgive me'." She took the flowers and went back into the house leaving the door open as an invitation for Jack to follow. He took off his cap and followed her into the kitchen. She arranged the flowers in a vase, and they filled the room almost at once with a heavenly scent.

Rosie considered Jack for a long moment.

"It's a cold night to be sleeping rough," she said. "You may sleep in the stable loft again if you wish."

"I'm forgiven then?" quizzed Jack carefully. He stepped further into the room and the candlelight illuminated the concern in his eyes. "I was a fool," he said. "I thought I was doing what was best for the boys. Rosie, I beg your forgiveness. In my haste I didn't stop to think that they were your adopted family and that I should have sought your opinion first."

"It is I who should be seeking forgiveness," she said. "I behaved badly. You have done nothing but good." She shifted uncomfortably. "When you grow up as independently as I have grown up, it is hard to tolerate change. It is hard to..." she hesitated, knowing that she was on the edge of words she might not be able to take back. "It is hard to be in someone's debt," she finished.

He took her hand very gently and put her fingers to his lips. "Rosie Potter, if only you knew," he said, "how very much more I am indebted to you."

Chapter Five

It was nearly Christmas and large goose feather snowflakes flurried and darted. The market awnings were quickly cloaked in a crisp layer of glistening white. Rosie tried to remember that she was nineteen years of age and could no longer scamper around like an excited child. Secretly she couldn't resist sticking her tongue out and catching stray flakes on her tongue. She tilted her face to the sky and tried to let the flakes land on her hair and lashes. She loved snow and she loved Christmas.

Will, Charlie and Sparrow had been as good as their word. They had come frequently to visit Rosie. Each time she saw them they seemed a little more grown up.

"Reading's easy!" Will had told her. "Don't know why I ever thought it was only clever folks what could read."

"But you are clever!" Rosie had insisted.

"Straight away we went to the top of the class for arithmetic," Charlie had added.

"Well that's not a surprise," Rosie had felt a lump of pride in her throat. "All that mental arithmetic you have done on the barrows. You were bound to be top of the class."

"We do miss the market though," Sparrow had said," and ... and ... you and Ma' Maggie," he had added embarrassedly.

It had been music to Rosie's ears, and she had scooped him up in a hug. "Once school has finished," she had told him, "you must come and help me sell Christmas wreaths. I will share the profits."

Rosie had taught Jack how to make the bases for her Christmas wreaths, and he had proved a quick learner. He had sat up night after night lumping together large wreaths of sphagnum moss and wiring them tightly. Then Rosie had decorated them with holly, spruce, berries, cones and crimson ribbon.

"We make a good team," Jack had observed standing back to admire their artistry. Rosie had nodded approval. She remembered the previous Christmas when she had managed to make only half the number of wreaths. This year she would make a handsome profit.

Now the wreaths hung all around her barrow. The smell of fresh conifer and roasting chestnuts mingled in the snow leaden air.

Jack marched around the market with wreaths on each arm. "Finest Christmas wreaths," he shouted. "Get your wreaths from Rosie Potter."

Jack had a great presence about him, and heads began to turn, especially women's heads noticed Rosie with a tinge of jealousy. Jack was taller than other men and more powerful. His dark looks and brilliant eyes were commanding. What woman wouldn't look twice.

Jack was quick to notice when he had gained attention, and even quicker to make a sale.

"Wreaths fit for royalty," shouted Jack. Then as if by some strange twist of fate, it really did seem as if royalty had arrived at their east end market. A murmur rippled through the crowd and a frisson of excitement. Rosie looked to where the crowds had parted and saw a man and a child walking together. The child was dressed for all the world like a princess in deep red velvet with a matching bonnet and fur muff. Her father walked ahead looking down at the market below his aristocratic nose. He was tall and his Saville row top hat made him look taller still. He was wearing a long woollen coat with a fur collar, and he tapped a gold tipped walking cane as he stepped through the impacting snow. A porter laden with purchases and a shiny faced nanny walked closely by the little girl who had a tendency to dart left and right to examine each stall. It was as though the child had not seen anything of the world before and everything intrigued her. Behind the incongruous party, like a flock of seagulls following a rich ship, a group of small beggar boys followed with outstretched grubby hands. The aristocratic father threw a handful of ha'pennies across the ice capped cobbles but more in a gesture to be rid of the beggars rather than any show of charity.

Rosie span round looking for Jack. This family would most certainly buy one of her wreaths and they would probably pay double the price. But to Rosie's astonishment Jack was nowhere to be seen.

"He went that way," said Ma' Maggie pointing in the opposite direction to the advancing family. "He looked in a hurry."

Rosie frowned. It wasn't like Jack to miss a business opportunity. But if Rosie had worried that the wealthy family might miss out her barrow, she needn't have done. The man with the top hat and gold tipped walking cane seemed almost to be making a bee line for her barrow.

"Are you Rosie Potter?" the man enquired.

"That's what it says on the barrow," said Rosie. "The very same." The child's nanny gave a faint smile as though admiring Rosie's style, but the man remained expressionless.

"Have you bought a Christmas wreath yet sir?" asked Rosie. "You won't find any finer than these."

The man opened his wallet and Rosie noticed at once that it was bursting at its seams. "And you'll be wanting some mistletoe sir," she said nodding towards the buckets of long twisting stems with their small white berries.

The porter who had had the grave misfortune of accompanying the father and daughter on their expedition wilted as Rosie added a wreath and two bunches of mistletoe to the pile he was carrying which already included a small Christmas tree and a goose.

"Did you make all these wreaths on your own?" asked the man tucking his wallet back into his coat.

Rosie looked back at him evenly. It seemed like an innocent enough question but working on the market had taught her never to divulge anything to anyone. "Yes," she replied, "I'm resourceful me."

Was it her imagination, or did the man's expression seem to cloud? He regarded her coolly for a moment and then turned on his heel.

"Thank you Rosie Potter," called the small girl over her shoulder as though to make up for her father's lack of manners.

Rosie watched as the little entourage disappeared back into the crowd like some exotic mirage.

"Funny that wasn't it?" said Ma' Maggie. "It was as though they were seeking you out. The man asked for you by name. Why would he be doing that?"

Rosie shrugged. "My reputation goes before me," she boasted. "Everyone's heard of Rosie Potter."

It was a good hour before Jack returned to the barrow and there was an unmistakable smell of alcohol on his breath.

"Where did you get to?" accused Rosie. "There was a toff here with money. You were needed."

"Was that all the toff wanted?" asked Jack unsettled. "Did you miss a sale?"

"Well no but..." She switched tack. "And alcohol on your breath. What time of day is this for there to be alcohol on your breath? And where did you get the money might I ask?"

"Anyone would think she was your missus!" shouted the farrier from a nearby stall selling rabbit fur muffs and mittens.

Rosie flushed crimson. It was true. She was beginning to treat Jack with all the familiarity of a wife.

Jack took both ends of her shawl and pulled her towards him, alcohol lending him a little confidence. "Rosie Potter," he said. "It's nearly Christmas and we haven't done anything to celebrate the season. What say you and I take a walk in the park? They say there's a concert band playing in the band stand and everyone will be there."

For some reason Rosie felt uncharacteristically shy. She had no difficulty in sitting by his side all night making wreaths by candlelight, but walking with him to the park to listen to a concert felt very different.

Rosie shook her head firmly. "I couldn't possibly," she protested. "There are ten wreaths left to sell. They'll not sell when Christmas is done and then all our work will have been wasted."

"I'll sell them for you," piped up Ma' Maggie with a mischievous twinkle. "And I'll keep an eye on the barrow until you get back."

"There, that's all settled," said Jack and he linked Rosie's arm companionably and dragged her away.

"You watch him!" cackled Ma' Maggie affectionately. "He's slippery that one. Slippery as one of Ed's eels."

The park was filled with men women and rosy cheeked children all skipping along in the snow. The gas lamps were lit against a leaden sky and a fresh snowfall was weighting down the boughs of the trees. The familiar shapes of benches, park rollers and rowing boats had been transformed by heaps of snow into eerie mammoths.

In the midst of the scene stood the bandstand festooned with lanterns and garlands of holly. The bandsmen, dressed in suits, bow ties and overcoats were breathing warm air into trumpets and flutes ready to tune up.

The conductor, who had cultivated a moustache that went on for at least two inches on either side of his mouth, tapped his baton for attention. He wore a bright red cummerbund which looked like it couldn't decide which side of his large belly to sit. "Ladies and Gentlemen," he boomed. "A merry Christmas to you one and all."

There was a huge cheer from the crowd.

"I've never been to a concert before," mouthed Rosie feeling the need to whisper.

"What never?" said Jack his eyes shooting wide in astonishment.

She shook her head.

"You need initiating," he said. "They'll start with a set of Viennese waltzes to begin with, and people will dance."

"Dance!" repeated Rosie horrified. "But I've never danced. I don't know how."

"Never danced!" Jack was incredulous. "Then I shall teach you."

Rosie's horror intensified. "No please! I shall be dreadful at it."

The conductor's baton rose and fell and the music swooped. Jack took Rosie's hand and gave a slight bow. "Follow me," he said. "Start with your right foot. One two three, one two three..."

Rosie began to move with the music staring very hard at her feet.

"You don't need to look so hard at your feet," laughed Jack, "they won't disappear. Keep your chin up. Look into my face."

She looked into his face and her pulse began to quicken. She must concentrate on the music. 'One two three. One two three.' Suddenly the music transitioned into a polka.

"This is a little faster and a little harder," laughed Jack, "but you can do it. Hop onto your right and then your left. Now a skip. Hop skip. Hop skip."

Rosie suddenly noticed the curious glances Jack was attracting. He was easily the best dancer. He danced as though he had been born to it, as though he had frequented all the best ballrooms in Vienna. She wondered where he had learned.

"I need to stop!" she panted at length. "I need to rest."

Jack stopped at once. He was laughing down at her and holding her tightly. He kept hold until she had regained her balance. "Wait here!" he commanded, and he disappeared into the crowd. He returned with two steaming cups of mulled wine. "Sip it," he said seeming to know that she had not drunk wine before. She sipped it all the way down to the bottom and felt a giddy warmth descending all the way down to her toes.

"Merry Christmas Rosie Potter," he said and then he kissed her. Somewhere at the edge of her world the concert band was playing 'Hark the Herald Angels Sing,' but all she knew was the warm kiss that pressed for more and awakened a tingling of passion that grew and grew.

She stepped back suddenly aware of the impropriety of a kiss in a public place. "I think I should go back now," she said.

Jack smiled down at her and his hands still held her face. "You get back into the warmth of the house," said Jack. "I shall go back and fetch the barrow and follow on."

Rosie nodded gratefully. The dancing followed by the wine and the kiss had made her giddy.

She fled off into the snow. The gas lamps that lined the paths from the bandstand shone extra brightly across the snow. She slipped and slithered out of the park and across the icy road like an over excited child. The world was suddenly a wonderful place. It felt as though Jack could do no wrong. Everything he did was tinged with a special magic. He had turned around the lives of the barrow boys and now he was turning her life around too. It occurred to her that she had hardly given Arthur Tipple a thought all day. Her only thoughts had been of Jack. Could she be falling in love? She must keep her head. She remembered Ma' Maggie's words. 'Be careful,' the old lady had warned. "He's slippery that one, as slippery as one of Ed's eels."

By the time Rosie had reached her street the moon had settled over the chimney pots. Some of the pots were already belching smoke, but not Rosie's since she hadn't been home all day. She hitched up her skirts, retrieved the front door key and let herself in. She was expecting the house to be in complete darkness, but it wasn't. There was a glow from the kitchen, the glow of a single candle. Rosie stopped in her tracks. She had not left a candle alight; she was sure of it. With a painful thump her heart missed a beat. There was a man in the room. The man was sitting in the dark and silence of her kitchen and he was rising to her feet as she entered.

"Who are you?" she demanded trying not to show fear. "How dare you enter my house. I will call the police at once."

"I apologise if I have frightened you Miss Potter," said the man moving towards the candle and not sounding one bit apologetic. "I mean you no harm."

Then as the man moved towards the light, Rosie recognised who he was. He was the rich man who had visited her barrow earlier that day and bought a Christmas wreath.

Rosie was overtaken by a terrible sense of foreboding. "I don't know what you want," she said, "and I have no interest. You have broken into my house, and I want you to leave this minute."

The man sat down at the table and surveyed her with something verging on scorn. He gave an unpleasant laugh. "Only it's not your house is it?" he said. "I might have forced the lock on the door from the yard but that doesn't make me a burglar in the eyes of the law. The house Miss Potter, was bought with my money."

Rosie let the words sink in for a moment but they made no sense.

"My son, John Beaumont bought the house," said the man softly, "but he bought it with my money. I think that entitles me to sit in your kitchen, don't you?"

"I don't know any John Beaumont," shrugged Rosie. "I don't know who you are or what you're talking about. I want you to leave."

"But you do know my son and it appears you know him very well." The man gave Rosie a twisted sort of smile fully aware of the bombshell he was about to drop into her world. "You know my son as Jack!"

"Jack?" Rosie's head reeled. Shock numbed her face and fingers.

"Jack is my son," persisted the man fixing her with steely grey eyes. "His real name is John Beaumont."

"No!" Rosie shook her head fiercely. "Jack is obviously not your son. He can't be."

"Why?" said the man. "Because he has traded his fine clothes for rags?" He gave a short laugh. "My son has done a splendid job of taking you in hasn't he?"

Rosie began to tremble violently, whether from the cold or shock she wasn't sure. Of course, she was forced to concede, it wouldn't be the first time she had been taken in by a man. She remembered the lies Arthur had spun. She remembered the lies she had been so eager to believe. Was she so gullible?

"But that's my son all over," said the man and he drummed his fingers listlessly on the top of his walking cane. "I brought him up to be a gentleman. I taught him to read the finest books and understand the theories of Galileo and Copernicus. I taught him to box and to fence. I taught him what foods to appreciate and what fine wines to drink. I taught him how to treat servants and how to run a country estate with fifteen acres of tenanted farmland. I bought him up to succeed me." He cast Rosie a suddenly malicious look. "I brought him up to marry the daughter of my second cousin, the very beautiful and accomplished Lady Eleanor. The wedding will go ahead as soon as my son has faced up to his responsibilities and returned to Beaumont."   Rosie's legs suddenly felt as though they could hold her no longer. She sat down with a bump. "I don't believe you," she managed. "You're mistaken."

"I am Lord Leopold Beaumont, Fifth Earl of Beaumont, and if everything goes to plan, my son John will be Sixth Earl of Beaumont. It is what he was born to do. Did you really know nothing of it? Did John never speak of the woman he was to marry, the woman who would stand by his side as Lady Eleanor Beaumont?" The man's eyebrows rose fractionally above the rim of his monocle. "He and Lady Eleanor have been courting for years and everything was well until this sudden flight of fancy."

Rosie felt tears pricking under her lashes and she forced them back.

"Then one morning John wasn't to be found," said Leopold Beaumont. "Nobody knew what to think. He had gone out riding and his horse came back unsaddled. I feared an accident and I involved the local constabulary. The constabulary discovered very quickly a notorious beggar in the next town wearing John's clothes. At first I believed the beggar had attacked and robbed my son, but that seemed unlikely."

Rosie remembered how well Jack had fought the Heneghan brothers. It seemed unlikely to her too.

"The beggar told the constabulary that my son had traded his rich clothes for the beggar's rags. Suddenly it was clear. My son had traded his identity for whatever reason I could scarcely fathom. I hired an investigator. It was only a question of time before we would trace my son's whereabouts. He might have traded his clothes, but he had not traded his bank account into which I pay a handsome monthly sum. Before long it was easy to trace cheques made to schools for barrow boys, medical fees for a young boy with palsy, and this house Miss Potter. My son bought this house outright. Did he not think the paper trail would lead directly to your doorstep? After that it was a simple exercise in surveillance."

From somewhere behind Rosie's head there was a sudden draft, and the candle flickered. Without having to turn around Rosie knew that Jack was standing behind her. Leopold Beaumont's eyes locked with his son's.

"It appears that my son does not want the title to which he was born," went on Lord Beaumont. "More to the point, my son does not want to face up to his responsibilities. My son lacks backbone. My son is a coward."

"I am not a coward," bit back Jack softly. "I am not afraid of responsibility. I wanted different responsibilities, responsibilities of my own making. I wanted a life of my own choosing. My life has been carved out for me from the moment I first drew breath. What subjects I should study. What friends I should make. What career I should follow. What woman I should marry."

Rosie closed her eyes. So it was all true. Her Jack, the man she had been growing to love, was not the man he had pretended to be.

"I was stifled," said Jack. "I wanted to know what it was like to be independent, at liberty to make my own choices."

"And this is independence?" snorted Jack's father waving his hand at the small kitchen with its peeling walls. "You retained your savings, your bank account and your allowance. You have lived on my money. You have merely played at being independent and no more. How easy it must have been to pander to the popularity afforded by a handful of beggar boys. How good it must have felt to pay for schools and medicines and an expensive doctor on my money."

"Father, you have said enough," said Jack in a dangerous sort of voice.

"You exchanged your clothes for rags not because you wanted to be independent," went on his father relentlessly, "but because you did not wish to live up to your responsibilities."

"Father," repeated Jack. "Stop! You have said more than enough."

"With privilege comes responsibility," said Lord Beaumont. "The men and women who live and work on the estate will one day rely upon you. I am ashamed that you think you can turn your back on your destiny."

"Father stop!"

"I am ashamed that you should have abandoned Lady Eleanor without so much as a note. She is worth ten of you. You could not live up to her. I am ashamed to call you my son."

"STOP!" Jack's knuckles were white in his fists. His face was contorted with anger.

But Jack's father did not relent. He got up from his chair and faced his son. "Is this what you want John?" he asked. "Are you really prepared to trade a title, a manor house and a fifteen-acre estate to live in this hovel? Are you prepared to break off your engagement to Lady Eleanor for a guttersnipe who scrapes a living from selling holly boughs scavenged from cemeteries?"

Rosie gasped to hear herself described as a guttersnipe.

Jack snapped! He leapt forward and grabbed his father by the throat. "You take that back damn you!"

There was an unmistakable look of triumph in Lord Beaumont's face. He rose slowly to his feet and Jack released his grip knowing that he had been wrong to lay hands on his father and lowered his eyes.

"I shall leave now," said Jack's father. "I will expect you back home by the weekend. If you are not back by the weekend, I will cut off your inheritance and the allowance that you have been enjoying at my expense. That way you will learn independence the hard way."

"Then I shall learn the hard way and gladly," said Jack in a low voice. "You are a tyrant and a bully, and I will not live another day under your roof."

Lord Beaumont did not flinch at his son's insult. He gave him a long steady look. "If you do not return, the inheritance with all its responsibility and privilege will pass to your sister."

"Martha?" Jack gestured disbelief. "Martha is barely twelve. How could Martha run the estate?"

"I will find her a fine husband," said Lord Beaumont. "A husband capable of running the manor and the farmland. Maybe Martha is made of sterner stuff than you."

"You cannot inflict that on Martha," said Jack genuinely appalled. "Martha is a child. She needs to make her own choices. She needs to choose her own husband when she is old enough to choose."

"The decision is yours," shrugged Jack's father. He pulled on his gloves ready to depart. "You may leave this house to this woman if you wish," he gestured towards Rosie without meeting her eye. "I expect you owe it to her."

The implication that Rosie might have earned the house by compromising her virtue was suddenly more than Rosie could bear. She opened her mouth to speak but nothing came out. Her head felt suddenly light, and her world span out of control. The floor came up fast to meet her and she was overtaken by a thick silence.

Chapter Six

Every bone in her body told Rosie that she had spent the night on the kitchen settle. The kitchen was curiously bright, and Rosie didn't have to lean over and scratch the ice that had formed on the inside of the windows to know that there had been a fresh snowfall. She could hear the crackle of the kitchen fire and knew that Jack was sitting by her side. He looked down at her, his usually good-humoured face grey and grizzled with angst and lack of sleep.

Her waking memory was of the kiss they had shared. Her stomach lurched at the memory. The waking memory was quickly overtaken by the memory of Leopold Beaumont's unpleasant visit. The dreadful revelations tumbled back into her consciousness, and she struggled to sit up.

Jack tried to push her back gently onto the cushions. "Stay where you are," he ordered. "I will make some sweet tea."

Rosie frowned up at him. "I'm surprised you're still here," she said. "Your father made it clear you must return."

Jack was silent for a moment as though he wasn't sure whether or not to ask his next question. "And you Rosie," he said. "Do you want me to go?"

Her lip trembled. "I hardly know who you are," she said. "You made me trust you. Now I know I trusted in a lie."

"I have never lied to you," protested Jack.

"You pretended you were a homeless beggar."

"I never pretended to be homeless," said Jack. "You assumed I was homeless."

"John Beaumont," said Rosie finding his real name hard to use. "The minute you dressed in rags and posed as someone that you were not, you were living a lie."

"It was the only way I could escape my father's tyranny," said Jack looking down at his hands. "But I never set out to deceive."

"You set out to deceive every bit as much as Arthur Tipple set out to deceive," snapped Rosie.

Jack's face clouded in sudden anger, and he clenched his fingers into his fists. "Do not compare me with Arthur Tipple," he ground out. "He never intended to stand by your side whereas I will never leave your side."

Rosie closed her eyes. She wanted to believe him, but she knew that it could come to nothing. "And what of your responsibilities?" she asked softly. "What about all the people that rely upon you? What about your inheritance?"

"I don't care tuppence ha'penny for the inheritance," said Jack. "I will gladly give it all up to stay with you."

"And what of Lady Eleanor?"

"She is a very fine woman," said Jack. He lowered his eyes. "She deserves better than me."

Rosie grimaced. She'd hoped for a different answer. "And what of your sister?" said Rosie. "Would you see her married off as a child bride to an older man that she does not love to run the estate that you should be running? It seems as though you have little choice."

Jack turned his back. It seemed he had no answer to this.

"I'm going to take the barrow to market," said Rosie. "When I return, I do not expect you to be here."

Rosie picked up her cloak and tied it tightly around her shoulders. She hesitated for a moment at the door. She found that she could not bring herself to bid him farewell, so she stepped out into the snow without saying anything at all. Perhaps Jack could not bid farewell either, because he remained with his back turned, and when Rosie returned hours later, he had gone.

"Gone?" said Ma' Maggie in askance.

Rosie was tying what was left of her Christmas wreaths around her barrow and arranging swathes of mistletoe.

"He was not what he seemed," explained Rosie, and she described the terrible evening where Lord Leopold Beaumont, Fifth Earl of Beaumont had visited. "It appears Jack lied to me every bit as much as Arthur Tipple lied," frowned Rosie her lip trembling all over again.

Ma' Maggie smiled faintly. "Do not be too harsh on him Rosie Potter," she said. "He may have concealed the truth of who he was but what choice did he have? I know a good man when I see one," she went on. "You cannot let him go."

"If only it was as simple as that," said Rosie. "He is engaged to be married to the daughter of his father's cousin, Lady Eleanor. The farmers and tenants will rely upon Jack to run the estate. Worse, if Jack does not take up the running of Beaumont, his father will have his twelve-year-old daughter married to a man she does not love in order to manage the estate."

Ma' Maggie twisted the tops of the chestnut cones thoughtfully and arranged them in a basket. "I don't pretend to have an answer," she said, "but that man rescued us from the Heneghans and he touched all of our lives. Now it's our turn. We have to rescue Jack from a loveless marriage and from a future he does not want."

"But how!" frowned Rosie. "There is no honourable way out of the ultimatums Jack's father has made."

"You'll think of a way," cackled Ma' Maggie. "You're Rosie Potter and Rosie Potter always thinks of a way."

Christmas day dawned cold and grey. Will and Charlie's mother had invited Rosie for Christmas dinner. Rosie had thanked her but pretended to have had a prior invitation. In truth she was in no mood for Christmas fun and games. She sat in her kitchen trying to keep warm over the last lumps of coal. She had been alone every Christmas since the death of her father, but this Christmas she felt lonelier than ever before. She pulled on her best cloak, put on a bonnet that she only wore for Christmas and set off for church. Along the cobbled streets and narrow pavements, the snow was beginning to thaw. Children all in their Christmas best were slipping to church clutching their parents' hands. The church bell was beginning to toll an invitation to all to come and sing Christmas carols and listen again to the Christmas story. It seemed that the whole world was filled with Christmas joy. Everyone but Rosie Potter. Rosie stepped through the slush with a heavy heart. She had fantasised that she might be walking to church with Jack at her side, yet here she was alone again. Misery washed over her. Then it came to her in an epiphany moment. She loved him. She loved him with every ounce of her being. Ma' Maggie was right. She could not let him go. She needed to rescue him from a loveless marriage and a future he did not want just as he had rescued her little barrow family. She knew she must do it, but she didn't know how.

Rosie stepped inside the church strangely reassured by its old familiar smells of musty kneelers and leather-bound hymn books. At the front, the vicar was talking about the shepherds on that very first Christmas. The altar boys were mouthing the worlds to 'While Shepherds Watched' and 'Hark the Angels'. In front of her there was a sea of Christmas bonnets and top hats. Everyone seemed to be part of a family, everyone but her.

Rosie raised her eyes to the massive stained-glass windows and made a silent prayer. She asked God for a way to rescue Jack. She asked for a way forward. She asked for a miracle. The vicar continued to tell the story of the first Christmas, and the altar boys continued to giggle and nudge each other but God remained silent.

The service came to an end and the vicar hurried to shake everyone's hand as they tumbled back out into the cold. Everyone was standing on the church steps wishing each other a merry Christmas. Children were racing and tugging, keen to get home for toys and Christmas dinner. Rosie tried to side-step the crowds when a boy looking strangely familiar lurched towards her. He was well dressed though walking with a leg brace. It was Eddie.

Rosie gave a squeal of delight and threw her arms around him in a big hug.

"Eddie!" she cried. "I hardly recognised you. You have grown so big and strong and look so well."

Eddie was laughing happily. Behind him a man in a dark wool coat and a woman with neatly coiffed hair and a kind smile came up to support the boy.

"Rosie," said the woman extending a gloved handshake. "You might not recognise us, but we know all about you."

The man raised his hat. "I'm Doctor Blake," he said. "This is my wife, Grace."

"We were happy to find you here this morning," said Grace. "Would you walk with us? We're going to put some flowers on Eddie's grandfather's grave."

"Grave!" echoed Rosie in horror. "I'm sorry! I didn't know."

"Yes a while ago," said Grace sadly, "and so my husband and I have decided to adopt Eddie."

"We have become very attached to the boy," said the doctor, "and dedicated to making him well."

The doctor pushed open the little metal gate into the church yard and held it open for his wife, Rosie and Eddie. Snowdrops were already pushing brave little heads up through the snow. Each gravestone wore a little mop cap of melting snow. Eddie limped over to his grandfather's stone and Grace handed him a bunch of lilies to place on the plinth.

Grace watched her new son-to-be fondly. "Rosie," she said. "We want to have Eddie baptised because he has never had a baptism. We wondered if you would do us the very great honour of being Godmother. I realise you may need time to think about it."

Rosie flushed pink. "Of course I don't need to think about it," she cried. "It would be a very great honour to be Eddie's Godmother. I will take the responsibility very seriously." She thought for a moment. "Who will be Godfather?" she asked.

"My husband's brother," said Grace.

Rosie sagged with disappointment. For a wild moment she had hoped that Eddie's new parents might have asked Jack to be Godfather. After all it had been Jack who had paid for Eddie's medical care and first introduced Eddie to the doctor and his wife.

Grace seemed to read Rosie's mind. "We wanted Jack to be Godfather, but the minister says that Godparents themselves must be baptised, and it appears that there is no record of Jack being baptised."

Rosie scrunched her face in puzzlement. "I'm surprised," she said. "I know that Jack possessed a Bible and that he attended Sunday services. It's strange that he was never baptised."

Grace gave Rosie a careful look. "I did not say that he was not baptised," she said. "I said that we could not find evidence of it. We know from his cheques that Jack's full name is John Beaumont and so we traced him to his local church. But the vicar there told us that the page in the register upon which Jack's baptism would have been recorded had been carefully removed."

"Removed?"

"Yes," said Grace. "Cut from the register with a knife."

Rosie let the words sink in for a moment. "As though someone was trying to hide something?" she asked.

Grace shrugged. "Who knows. There would have been more than one baptism entry on the missing page, so perhaps we shouldn't read too much into it."

As if on cue, the grey clouds parted, and a ray of struggling sunlight spread fingers of light across the gravestones. Rosie looked up at where the clouds had separated, and her mind began to race. Somehow, she had to find what was recorded on Jack's missing baptism entry. She had to know if someone was trying to hide something. If there was a secret around Jack's birth, she would find it.

"Penny for 'em?" said Ma' Maggie. Rosie broke from her daydreaming, suddenly aware that she had allowed at least ten or so potential customers to wander by her barrow without making a single sale.

Rosie gave a brief smile. "My thoughts aren't worth a penny," she said sadly.

"What's happened to the old Rosie Potter?" said Ma' Maggie. "The old Rosie Potter would have had a plan by now to win back the man she loved."

Rosie sighed. "I have half a plan," she said. "But only half a plan." She told Ma' Maggie about her conversation with the doctor's wife. She told the old lady how she had been asked to be Eddie's Godmother. It had been the doctor's plan to ask Jack to be Godfather. It was then that it had come to light that someone had taken great pains to remove the record of Jack's baptism from the church register.

"As though someone had something to hide," concluded Rosie. "Maggie, what if there is some family secret? What if there is a family secret that I could use to free Jack from his father's tyranny?"

Ma' Maggie gave Rosie a sympathetic look. "As you say," she said. "You only have half a plan. There would have been more than one baptism on the missing page, at least three other baptisms. Even if there was a family secret to discover, however will you discover it?"

Rosie scowled. "You were the one who said I should rescue Jack in the same way that he rescued us. I'm going to write to Beaumont Manor and find myself a position," said Rosie. "I shall go in disguise. Neither Leopold Beaumont nor his son Jack will recognise me. I'm Rosie Potter and I'm resourceful. If there's a family secret to discover, I am the one to find it."

Ma' Maggie began to cackle. "It's the most dreadful plan. It hasn't a chance of working. But a dreadful plan is better than no plan at all."

So Rosie drafted a letter in her best hand. She assumed the name 'Mrs Barton' and enquired after a position for any of her children who were of working age. She wrote in particular of her daughter who would make a very fine maid. Then she put Ma' Maggie's address on the top because she was afraid that someone at Beaumont might recognise her own address. Ten days later a letter arrived back and Ma' Maggie hurried to market waving it in the air jubilantly.

Rosie's heart gave an unpleasant thump to see the envelope with the Beaumont stamp. She fingered the small envelope nervously.

"Open it!" cried Ma' Maggie impatiently. "Read it quickly."

Rosie opened the letter quickly and scanned it. "It's from a Mr Montgomery," said Rosie. "He signs himself 'estate secretary'. He says that currently they have no vacancies for a maid, but they do have a position for a boy to help in the garden. He says that the boy should be fit and strong and used to working long hours in all sorts of weather."

"Oh well! That's that then," said Ma' Maggie disappointed.

Rosie continued to stare thoughtfully at the letter. "Well I'm fit and strong," she said, "and I'm certainly used to working long hours in all sorts of weather."

"But you're not a boy," said Ma' Maggie as though this basic piece of information might somehow have escaped Rosie's attention.

"But I'm as strong as a young boy," said Rosie thinking out loud. "And if I was dressed in a boy's clothes and boots, and if my hair was cut very short..."

Rosie snatched up the scissors she used to cut her flower stems and handed them to Ma' Maggie. "Maggie," she said sitting herself on an upturned crate. "Quickly! Cut my hair for me. Cut it as short as a boy."

Ma' Maggie's eyes shot wide in horror. "Not your beautiful long curls. Rosie you mustn't!"

Rosie gestured exasperation. "It will grow again," she said. "Come on quickly before I change my mind."

Slowly and reluctantly, Ma' Maggie took the scissors and began to cut Rosie's hair. The long glossy red curls fell onto the cobbles and blew away in the wind. A small group of astonished market goers stood and watched. Some gasped in horror and others began to laugh imagining that it might be some sort of publicity stunt.

"There," said Ma' Maggie when her work was done. "I can't get it any shorter than that."

Rosie ran her fingers through the silky tufts. "Do I look like a boy?" she asked.

"Not much," grinned Ma' Maggie. "I've not seen a boy with such long lashes, or so delicate a chin."

Rosie frowned. "I can make my face look grubby," she said. "I'm sure I can look like a boy. No one will know that I am really Rosie Potter, not even Jack."

Chapter Seven

Rosie stood at the gates of Beaumont Manor. She gaped in awe at the gateposts each topped with a stone urn overflowing with carved garlands and acanthus leaves. She had never seen gates so grand. The horse and cart that had given her a ride for the last ten miles of her journey clip-clopped into the distance. Rosie pushed her hands into the boy's coat pockets she was wearing. She was painfully aware that she had spent her last coppers on carriage fares and the boy's boots and cap she had bought as her guise. It dawned on her that if she didn't get the job, she had no money at all to get back to London.

Rosie pushed open the gates and they swung open easily on heavy well-oiled hinges.

"Oi! You boy!" A shout arrested Rosie's attention. Then came the sound of running footsteps. Rosie turned to find a young girl in a striped dress and apron carrying a basket of shopping. Rosie pulled her cap down further to hide her face. Could it be possible that her disguise had been discovered so quickly?

"Tradespeople don't go through the front gate," panted the girl. "Don't you know nothing? Follow me!"

Rosie followed the young maid further down the lane to a little side entrance.

"We have to go around the side of the house," the young girl explained. Then she threw Rosie a suspicious glance. "What's your business here?" she asked.

"I heard there was a job," said Rosie. "For a gardener's boy."

"Ah!" said the girl. "You might be too late. There were two boys here this morning for an interview." Then noticing Rosie's crestfallen face. "Or maybe not. The head gardener is very particular about who he takes on."

"And what is it like working here?" quizzed Rosie carefully.

"Oh we're all the very best of friends," said the girl cheerfully. "We look after each other the best we can. I'm Molly by the way," she said offering her hand.

"Hello Molly," said Rosie. "I'm..." she hesitated. "Thomas. Thomas Barton."

"We've already got a Thomas," said Molly comfortably. "You'll probably get Tom or Tommy."

"And what of the lords and ladies?" asked Rosie, keen to hear a mention of Jack.

"Oh don't worry about them," said Molly. "You'll never have cause to see them, unless you go thieving. Take my advice. Never cross the earl. He is a tyrant and a bully. He has a daughter, Martha. She's very sweet, but rarely allowed out. A prisoner I'd say! Then there's Lord Beaumont's son, John Beaumont." Molly glanced over her shoulder and lowered her voice to a confidential whisper. "Don't tell anyone I told you, but John Beaumont is to be married soon to Lady Eleanor. There'll be an engagement party in a week or two and then a big wedding. Take my advice and keep your nose clean, because the head of estates has declared that every loyal servant on the day of the wedding will be given a silver shilling to mark the occasion."

Rosie felt as though she had been punched in the gut. She had known that Lord Beaumont was planning a wedding, but she had not imagined that it would be so soon."

"And do the couple look very much in love?" Rosie couldn't help asking.

Molly threw back her head and shrieked with laughter. "What a very strange question for a young boy to ask?" she said.

Rosie bit her lip. If she didn't want to arouse suspicion, she must be careful to remember that she was a fifteen-year-old boy and not a nineteen-year-old young woman.

"Take my advice," said Molly, "and mind this." She tapped the side of her nose. "No one likes a nosey parker. Keep your mind on your work and you will do very nicely." She put down her baskets by the trades entrance and pointed at a little sand path that ran round the back of the house and into the trees. "Follow that path," she said. "It will take you to the walled gardens. You will find Mr Evans there."

Rosie lifted her cap and pulled it back down. "Thank you miss," he said and made off in the direction Molly had pointed.

"And take my advice," said Molly. "Stop at the water pump and wash your hands and face. Mr Evans is very particular. Good luck Tommy Barton."

Rosie wandered into the walled gardens. She looked in awe at the row upon row of boxed hedge beds and fruit trees, dormant because it was January but ready to leap into life. Beyond the beds, row upon row of greenhouses reflecting a cool January sun in their half open glass roof panels. Intrigued, Rosie walked along a winding path and peeped into the first greenhouse. She saw pots of flowers lined up on slatted wooden benches. She couldn't resist a closer look. She climbed the steps and into the greenhouse breathing in the warm damp smell of compost and of flowers that would not normally be growing in the British climate. She ran her fingers along the petals of exotic orchids and lilies in awe at how well they had grown out of season.

"What the...!"

Rose span round to find a man standing behind her. He was glowering down at her; a muscular bearded man with thick black eyebrows which were knitted together in ferocious disapproval.

"I'm sorry sir," stammered Rosie. "I know I shouldn't have stepped in uninvited, but the flowers were so beautiful..." She swallowed hard remembering the reason she was supposed to be there. "I was looking for Mr Evans. I was interested in the position of garden boy."

The man's ferocious disapproval relaxed a little. "And you like the flowers?" he asked.

"I've never seen so many flowers growing so well out of season sir," said Rosie.

"And do you know the flowers?" asked the man.

"Of course!" said Rosie forgetting again that she was supposed to be a fifteen-year-old boy. "Carnations, lilies, honeysuckle, peonies, camellias..."

"And do you have experience of growing flowers and of tending gardens?"

Rosie shook her head reluctantly. "No," she confessed, "but I have knowledge of selling them. I work on the barrows see," she explained. "But I would love to learn how to grow them." She walked along the rows of Amaranthus. "Imagine," she went on, "the possibility of selling all these to market wholesalers who would normally have to pay the mark up for steamship transport."

The man gave a bark of laughter. "You have a business mind," he said, "but that's not why we grow them. The earl's grandmother, God rest her soul, had the greenhouses erected so that she could always have fresh flowers in her home and fresh fruit. It's a tradition we uphold."

"There are a lot of flowers here simply to uphold a tradition," said Rosie and the man laughed again.

"I have to tell you," said the man, "that your job would not be about growing flowers. It's a labouring job. It's about sweeping up the dead leaves, turning the soil over and helping to keep the grass and hedges cut back."

"Of course," said Rosie. "If you could point me in the direction of Mr Evans, I will tell him that I am fit and strong and no stranger to hard work. I hope the position is still open and that I might have an interview."

"I am Mr Evans," said the man unexpectedly. "You will be pleased to know that the position is still open, and you have just passed the interview. You can put on an apron right now, fetch a barrow and start sweeping up the leaves around the lake.

"Hello Tom Barton," said Molly who was emptying a bucket of vegetable peelings into the same compost heap Rosie was emptying leaves. "I hear you got the job."

"News travels fast," grinned Rosie.

"I might see you now and then," said Molly. "The last garden boy used to bring fresh flowers and fruit up to the house and I would take them in."

"The last garden boy?" quizzed Rosie. "What happened to him?"

"He was caught thieving," said Molly matter-of-factly, "and the earl took a horse whip and beat him to an inch of his life."

Rosie felt the blood draining from her face. She felt sick to her core. She despised bullies with all her being. "Did no one stop him?" she asked quietly.

Molly shrugged. "The earl pays our wages," she said. "No one dares stand up to him. My advice is to stay out of his way."

"Does he have no wife?" asked Rosie wondering if the earl had no calming influence in his life.

"Died in childbirth twelve years ago," said Molly. "Apparently he was a nicer person when she was alive."

Rosie's mind raced. So Jack's mother had died giving birth to Martha. She found herself wondering why there was such an age gap between Jack and his younger sister. The earl's wife sounded like she might have been a nicer person than he was, yet Jack had once described his mother as 'distant'.

"Apparently," said Molly emptying the last bucket of peelings, "the earl was never the same again. He has kept her room exactly the way it was on the day she died." Molly dried her hands on her apron. "That's her room up there overlooking the lake," said Molly pointing up at a second-floor bay window with ornately decorated sandstone corbels. Rosie felt the hairs standing up on the back of her neck. It was unsettling to know that there was a room at the hall where time had stood still. She imagined the spirit of Lady Beaumont standing in the casement looking out over the lake that she had looked upon every day in life. She imagined the dead woman's spirit frozen in time watching the world passing her by.

Over the next days and weeks Rosie found herself working ten times harder than she had ever worked on the barrows. She took the attic above the farrier's cottage where the garden boy had lived before her. The old couple that lived there included breakfast in exchange for chores and a few odd jobs. During the day there was a gruelling schedule of sweeping the pathways, turning the compost, digging the soil and cleaning all the gardening tools. She had never worked as hard as this on the barrows. But as she worked, she quizzed everyone she met, determined to learn the secret that the missing baptism page had seemed to suggest. But if there was any family secret to be discovered it was well and truly buried. Everyone it seemed remembered the day the doctor and midwife had arrived in a carriage to deliver the birth of Martha, but nobody was old enough to remember the birth of Jack. By the by she learned of other things she had not set out to learn. She learned how cruel the Fifth Earl of Beaumont was. She learned how he beat servants for little or no reason. She learned how he had thrown servants out simply for rising late or not working fast enough leaving them homeless and destitute.

Rosie began to feel quietly disheartened. Worse, on more than one occasion she had spotted Jack and Lady Eleanor walking arm in arm in the garden and through the rose arbours. Rosie had pulled down her cap and pushed her wheelbarrow nearer for a closer look at her rival. She wished that she hadn't. If she had secretly hoped that Lady Eleanor would be plain, she was to be disappointed. Lady Eleanor was beautiful. Her hair was an amazing mass of golden and strawberry blonde curls. Her eyes were a deep earnest blue. Her face seemed permanently kind and smiling. Eleanor was looking attentively into Jack's face, and they were sharing such a deep conversation that neither noticed the grubby garden boy studying them so intensely. Rosie had known an urge to throw off her cap and race across the lawn. She had wanted to pull Jack into her arms and remind him it was she he had once loved. She was swamped in misery. Suddenly the loveless marriage Jack had described didn't seem so loveless after all. The family secret, even if there was one, seemed more and more impossible to uncover. Even if she did manage to uncover a secret, what difference would it make?

Rosie's thoughts began to return to London and the market. She was missing the camaraderie of the market, and she was missing her adopted family. Jack and Eleanor's pending engagement party was going to be more than Rosie could bear. Perhaps it was time for her to leave. Broodily she piled leaves into the barrow. Ma' Maggie's words came back to her. Jack had rescued them from the Heneghan brothers. It was up to her to rescue

Jack from his tyrant of a father. She loved him and she must do her best. If after she had helped him stand up to his father, he decided he wanted to marry Lady Eleanor after all, then that was something she would have to bear.

The day of the engagement party dawned cold but sunny. January crocuses and primroses were pushing their heads up all over the Beaumont Estate. Steady streams of trades people were making their way round to the side of the manor house with baskets of fruit and meat. Delicious smells of cake and sweet pastries filled the air.

An idea was slowly formulating in Rosie's mind. The only place she had not looked for answers was in the manor house itself. She remembered how Molly had pointed up at the bay window overlooking the lake. This had been Mary's room. This was the room the earl had kept exactly how it was since his wife's death. Did this mean it would still contain diaries and letters? Might Rosie even find the baptism page that had been removed from the register? It didn't seem at all likely, yet it was the only idea she had left.

If ever there was a day to creep undiscovered into the house this was it. There were trades people all over the house, cleaning the long casement windows, sweeping the grand staircase, polishing brasses and moving furniture to create a large ballroom space in which the nobility could dance. A garden boy delivering fruit or flowers would not look out of place.

Rosie's opportunity came when Mr Evans asked her to fill baskets with the largest and fullest blooms she could cut and take them up to the house. Molly and other maids had been charged with making up floral displays in the hall and ballroom. Rosie could picture exactly what the displays should look like. She knew exactly what flowers to cut. She filled six large baskets with peonies, roses, lilies and long fronds of fern for texture. Hesitantly she added some strong stems of purple iris. She wondered if Jack would look at them and remember that it was her favourite flower. She wondered if he would remember the flower's message of faith, trust, courage and valour. She wondered if he would remember the adversity they had both faced. She wondered if the memory would stir any hope that they could still find happiness together away from his father's tyranny. She lifted the baskets carefully onto the barrow and wheeled it round to the side entrance of the manor house. She looked into the kitchen where Molly was so busy peeling vegetables that she hardly gave Rosie a second look.

"Thank you Tom Barton," said Molly taking a knife to another potato and adding it the growing pile. "Leave the flowers in the scullery if you will where it's dark and cool."

Rosie took the baskets into the scullery and decanted some of the more delicate blooms into buckets of water to keep them fresh. Then instead of going back the way she had come through the kitchen, she slipped up the servants' staircase to the second floor. Her heart was thumping. She knew if she met anyone on route, she had absolutely no excuse to be there. She made her way along the second-floor corridor. It was lined with oil paintings of Beaumont ancestors, but she didn't stop to look. She reached the room at the end of the corridor. She knew that this must be the room with the bay window overlooking the lake. This was Mary's room. She turned the handle gently and peeped inside.

It was like stepping into a time capsule. Just as Molly had described, the room had been perfectly preserved. Mary's silk dressing gown was still laid across the end of the bed. The eiderdown was folded down as though Mary might return at any time soon. Her hairbrushes and perfumes were arranged neatly on the dressing table. In the window there was a small writing desk upon which stood an ink stand and a large vase of tulips. Mr

Evans sent white tulips up to the house every other day. Tulips had been Mary's favourite. Rosie smiled. Tulips were amongst her favourite flowers too. They were the only cut flowers to grow after they had been cut, and she loved the way they refused to be arranged, twisting their faces to the light as though reaching for a glimpse of heaven and rebelling against the artistry of the florist.

Rosie ventured to pull down the lid of the writing desk, but if she had hoped that the desk might be full of letters and diaries brimming with family secrets, she was to be disappointed. The desk was completely empty.

Rosie stood in the middle of the room enjoying its ambience and subtle scent. Against the far wall stood a wardrobe with a long oval looking glass in its door. Rosie opened the wardrobe door wondering why she should feel that she was invading the privacy of a woman long dead. She ran her hand along the fine array of dresses and gowns. Rosie had never been told what Jack's mother looked like, but she could imagine from her narrow waisted dresses how elegant she must have been.

Rosie's imaginings were rudely interrupted by a sharp tap from behind her and a shadow from the corner of her eye. She span around in a fright and then breathed easily again. She laughed at how the imagination could play tricks. For a moment she had imagined Mary's ghost standing behind her, indignant that a grubby garden boy should be surveying all her fine dresses. In truth the shadow was cast by a tall fir tree just outside the window and the tapping was not the light footstep of Mary's ghost but a tree branch tapping on the window.

Rosie decided it was time to go. This room she decided would not reveal any family secrets. But just then there came another sound. This time it was not a tree branch tapping against the window. This time it was not Rosie's imagination. This time it was the unmistakable sound of a man's footsteps coming slowly and heavily along the corridor. The footsteps were so close that Rosie knew for sure that the man was heading for this room.

In a panic, Rosie flung herself onto the floor and wriggled under the bed. She stayed there as still as a mouse hardly daring to breath, hoping against hope that the man would not enter this room. He did. The door opened and Jack's father, Earl Beaumont stepped in. From her hiding place Rosie could see the hems of his tweed trousers and polished brown leather shoes. As he moved across the room, Rosie could see him clearly. He stood with his back to the bed. He had a large bunch of white tulips and long tendrils of eucalyptus leaves draped over one arm. He changed the flowers for the ones in the vase. Then he crossed the room to the washstand, picked up a large jug of water and topped up the vase. Then he stood for a while as though in silent prayer. This was obviously something he did every day in memory of his dead wife. Rosie felt a twinge of sympathy. She would not have expected this of a man so feared by his family and by his servants. Then to Rosie's horror he came over to the bed and sat on it. The mattress creaked and dipped almost to the side of Rosie's head. She clasped her hands over her nose and mouth to silence her own breathing. She was inches away from the back of his polished heels. For the first time in her life she knew real terror. She remembered Molly telling of how the cruel earl had beaten the previous garden boy to an inch of his life. She began to pray. She closed her eyes tightly and prayed hard not to be discovered. Her heart was beating so hard that she imagined he must surely hear it. Then after what seemed to be an eternity, Earl Beaumont stood up and headed for the door.

Rosie had just allowed herself to breathe again when he stopped in his tracks as though he had noticed something. He walked back into the room. He stopped for a moment by the bed and Rosie closed her eyes and began to pray again. Then he went over to the wardrobe and closed the door. Rosie bit her lip. How stupid she had been to leave it open. Now the earl would surely know that someone had been into the room. The earl looked around briefly as though checking whether anything else might be out of order before leaving and closing the door behind him. Rosie stayed where she was for a moment listening hard for Earl Beaumont's retreating footsteps. Instead, she heard the sharp click of a key turning in the lock. The earl had taken the precaution of locking his wife's room. Maybe he suspected that a nosey maid had peeped inside his dead wife's wardrobe. Rosie waited until the earl's footsteps had faded until crawling out from beneath bed and trying the door handle. Her worst fears were confirmed. She was well and truly a prisoner.

Cautiously, Rosie stepped over to bay the window and peeped out from behind the heavy drapes. A prisoner in the bedchamber of the ghost of the late Lady Mary Beaumont. How, thought Rosie, had she got herself into such a pickle? It wasn't entirely impossible she decided, to climb out of the window. The fir tree was close enough to the decorative stone that ran around the foot of the bay for her to be able to step out into the branches. But it certainly wasn't possible in the clear light of day. There was already a steady trickle of guests arriving at the front of the manor house, and there was a steady stream of tradespeople and musicians arriving at the side of the house. A garden boy climbing from a second storey window would be spotted at once. She would need to wait until the light had faded and make her escape by darkness.

Rosie leaned her head against the window sash and watched the long train of guests arriving some on foot and others in elegant horse drawn carriages. Lady Eleanor was one of the first guests to arrive. She was wearing a beautiful champagne pink silk dress with a matching gown. Her long slender neck was draped in rubies and pearls. She was accompanied by an entourage of family and friends. Both the earl and his son stepped out to meet Eleanor and her family and Jack took his fiancée's hand in his and kissed her fingers before offering her his arm and leading her up the steps and into the house. It had only been a polite kiss but a kiss nonetheless. Rosie retreated from the window and sat down hard on the bed. She sat there for a long time trying hard not to cry. She closed her eyes and listened to the musicians in the ballroom below as they tuned up. Then she heard the strains of something that stirred a memory. The strings were playing a waltz. It was a waltz Rosie knew. She remembered the concert band playing it in the band stand on the night before Christmas Eve. She remembered Jack teaching her to dance. She stood up from the bed with her eyes still closed and stepped around the room. "One two three, one two three." She remembered Jack telling her to look up into his face and not down at her feet. Even with her eyes shut she could picture his laughing face and glittering eyes. She remembered the snowflakes on her cheeks and lashes. She remembered how he had kissed her. She remembered the warmth and urgency of the kiss and she wondered if it had meant as much to him as it had meant to her. She dug her fingernails into her palms until they hurt. She pictured Jack taking Eleanor in his arms and dancing the same dance with her.

This was torture. She must head back for London in the morning. There was nothing in this room that could point to a family secret. Perhaps after all it was up to Jack himself to stand up to his father; Jack and his new wife. There was nothing she could do to rescue Jack from the life he was choosing. Perhaps, she thought, he had never needed rescuing in the first place. Defeated, she threw herself down on the bed and cried herself to sleep.

Chapter Eight

Rosie awoke with a start. She stared up at an unfamiliar ceiling and struggled to make sense of her darkened surroundings. She wondered what had awakened her so suddenly. It was though the tail end of a dream had followed her into wakefulness. She fancied there had been someone in the room. It was though a shadow had moved quickly away from the bed. She was quite sure she had heard the swish of a dress.

Rosie jack-knifed into a sitting position her heart beating rapidly. She noticed straight away that a wind had arisen and that the curtains had blown into the room knocking the vase of tulips from the top of the desk onto the carpet below. Fortunately, the glass had not smashed but the water was escaping fast. For the second time Rosie had stern words with herself at giving way to fancy. For the second time she had half fancied that Mary's ghost was in the room looking down at her. Rosie jumped up and rescued the vase. She set it upright and returned the tulips to the little water that remained. Then she took a handkerchief from her pocket and dabbed at the puddle beneath the desk.

It was whilst she was kneeling on the floor with her head under the desk mopping up the spill that she spotted something she would never have spotted if the tulips hadn't have blown over. Behind each of the front legs of the desk was a tiny brass clasp. Rosie stared for a moment before gently releasing the tiny clasps. As if by magic a secret drawer slid forward on well-engineered springs. Rosie's breath caught in her throat. The secret drawer was lined in neatly arranged bundles of letters and a small gold edged velvet backed diary. Rosie knew an involuntary frisson shoot through her veins. Could Mary's ghost have shown her how to open the desk? Was Mary's ghost leading her to the revelation that would help free Jack of the life his father had chosen for him? Rosie sat at the desk and sifted through the pages of the diary. The light outside was fading fast and she knew that she must read quickly. Below her there came the music and laughter of a party still in full swing, but she managed to shut it out.

A faded pink ribbon marked the page on which Mary had last written. It was the page that marked the birth of her daughter Martha. "I am happier than I ever remember," read Rosie. "We have decided upon the name of Martha, and although every new parent declares it, she really is the most beautiful child." Rosie turned the page curiously. "But the day is tinged with a little sadness," went on the entry. "When I look upon poor John, I have to confess an even greater regret than I felt before." Rosie stared long and hard at the words as though re-reading them might reveal some further meaning. She read on but there were no further mentions of John Beaumont. "Awaiting a visit from the doctor," read the last entry. "Feeling very weak and cannot breast feed." The next pages were blank. Rosie felt a lump in her throat. It was with incredible sadness she realised that she was reading the last words Mary had ever written.

Rosie turned her attention to the letters. There was one bundle tied in ribbon together with a pressed rose, once a vibrant red but now a faded pink. These were love letters from the earl, each one in Lord Beaumont's characteristic Scorpio scrawl and signed 'Forever Leopold.' Rosie shuddered. She couldn't imagine the earl ever being romantic or capable of affection. She hastily retied them and picked up another bundle. The letters in this bundle were all from someone called Dorothea. Rosie looked at the address in puzzlement. 'Blenheim Cottage'. She recognised the address. It was less than a mile away. Why write so many letters to someone in such easy walking distance? Then as Rosie turned the pages, she spotted the name 'John'. She spotted it lots of times. Slowly she understood that all the letters were about her Jack.

"I have made John a little red riding jacket," read one of the letters. "I wonder if I might bring it up to the house and whether you would allow John to wear it," read the letter.

"I am sad beyond words," read another letter, "that Leopold has taken to disciplining the boy. I have spoken with George and he too is gravely concerned. No one knows more than George that Leopold has a wicked temper. I urge you to stand up for yourself Mary, and I urge you to stand up for the boy."

Rosie re-read the letter carefully. Who was George? What relationship was he to John's father, Leopold? The letters offered no more clues to George's identity, but plenty more mention of Leopold's temper.

"I write again with heartfelt concern," read Dorothea's next letter. "I have cried to know that he would take a rod to John. Remember that George and I are not far away if you need us. If we need to, we will come and fetch the boy."

The line jumped out at Rosie. ".... We will come and fetch the boy." She read it over and over. What right would George and Dorothea have to come and fetch the boy, unless.... unless?

The light was lost. Rosie could read no longer. She retied the letters in their ribbons and replaced them in the secret drawer exactly as she had found them. She had a strong feeling that she had stumbled upon the family secret. Could it be that George and Dorothea were Jack's legitimate parents? The letters didn't say so, but there was some compelling evidence. If this was true, it would certainly explain why Jack's baptism page would have been cut from the parish record. The baptism page would have revealed Jack's true parentage.

A stillness descended. The music had stopped. On the drive outside carriages scrunched over the gravel to collect the guests and take them home. It was nearly dark, and Rosie decided it was time make her escape. It was just dark enough not to be spotted. If she waited for complete darkness it would be hard to see hand and footholds as she climbed the tree. She lifted the window gently and climbed out onto the ledge. Very carefully she reached for the first branch of the tree and felt around gingerly for a foothold. The branches bent slightly under her weight and the greenery scratched her face and hands. She began to shake. She was a city girl. She had never climbed a tree before. She took a deep breath. She might never have climbed a tree before, but as a child she and her brother had shinned up and down enough drainpipes. How different could this be? One branch at a time. Slowly slowly!

Below her a couple of the last guests were leaving. Her heart skipped! One of the shadowy figures below was Jack. She recognised immediately his height and the sturdy set of his shoulders. He was helping a friend who was a little worse the wear for port and lemons into his carriage. Rosie couldn't resist leaning forward to catch a little more sight of the man she loved. Suddenly there was a sickening crack. The branch below her feet had snapped. Rosie's arms flailed wildly trying to find a branch to save her, but it was no good. She was falling. She landed on her back on the gravel below. The impact forced an involuntary groan from her lungs.

In a trice she was back up on her feet, but too late, Jack was striding in her direction his face like thunder. "You boy! Stop right there!" he shouted.

Rosie didn't stop. She didn't waste a second. Under no circumstances could she allow Jack to find out that the garden boy climbing from his mother's window on the day of his engagement party was Rosie Potter.

She ran like the wind. If she headed for the woodland that ran around the edge of the lake, she would be able to lose him. She had never run so fast, slipping and sliding through the long grasses that edged the lake.

"Stop boy!" Jack was shouting. "Stop thief or things will be the worse for you."

Rosie knew a moment of indignation. How dare he think her a thief! But then, what was he supposed to think? He had caught her climbing from his mother's window.

The woodland was yards away, but Rosie's escape was not to be. A long tangle of weeds knotted around her ankle and sent her flying. Before she knew it, Jack's strong arms were pinning her face down.

"Now let's see who you are." Jack turned her to face him and whipped off her cap.

Rosie blinked up at him breathing hard. Unhelpfully, the moon chose that exact moment to slide from behind a cloud illuminating her delicate features and tufts of glossy curls that had begun to grow back.

"Rosie?" Jack loosened his grip. He looked down into her face in total incredulity. "Am I dreaming?"

"Are....are you pleased to see me?" was all Rosie could think of to say.

He pulled her to her feet roughly. "What do you think you're doing?" he ground out.

This was not the reaction Rosie had dreamt or hoped for. He looked angry, thunderous even. The old easy-going smiling Jack she had known and loved was gone. Now, for all the world he was John Beaumont, Sixth Earl of Beaumont.'"

"I thought you'd be pleased," said Rosie fighting tears. "I ... I came to rescue you."

"Rescue me?" Jack ran long fingers through his hair. "What are you talking about?"

Rosie looked away. She had imagined he might take her in his arms and tell her that he had missed her and still loved her. She had imagined that he would thank her for coming all this way to free him from the tyranny of his father. Instead, he was speaking to her as though she were some kind of lunatic.

Jack rescued her cap and returned it to her head. "You have to get out of here," he said, "as soon as possible."

Holding Rosie's arm so tightly that she winced with pain, he steered her back towards the house.

"Jack listen," panted Rosie half running to keep up. "I think your so-called father is keeping the truth from you."

"Don't think to cross my father," said Jack. "You have no idea what he would do if he discovered you here. You have no idea what he is capable of."

Rosie stumbled as Jack led her back along the manicured hedges that shielded the view from the house. "But Jack," she said, "what if he is not your father? I think I might have discovered who your real father might be."

Jack seemed to hesitate but only fractionally. "Stop this," he said. "Stop this Rosie Potter. We shared a brief romance, but it is over. Love is more than a kiss in the snow."

If he had struck her it would not have hurt so much. "But if you are not his son," she persisted, "what is to keep you here? What sense of duty should you have for a man who is not your father?"

Jack's grip tightened and he seemed to lead her along the path all the faster. "I will take you up to the lodge where Lady Eleanor is staying until the wedding day. She will give you a room to stay in and she will give you a dress to wear instead of this ridiculous boy's garb. I will explain that you are the person who put a roof over my head in London. She is as kind and as gentle as the day is long, and she will not ask any difficult questions of you."

Rosie was appalled. She couldn't think of anything worse than accepting a room and a dress from the woman who was about to marry the man she loved. "Jack, please listen," she said. "There are letters. They speak of two people I believe to be your real parents, George and Dorothea."

"I will organise a carriage to take you back to London first thing in the morning," said Jack stubbornly refusing to meet her eye. "You must never come here again."

"At least speak to them," persisted Rosie. "They live less than a mile away at Blenheim Cottage. Find out for yourself if they are your real parents."

Jack stopped in his tracks for a moment and turned to face her directly. He took her shoulders and shook her. "And what if they are?" he said. "What difference would it make? Even if not blood related, Martha is still my sister. I have to stay and protect her. She relies upon me. Regardless of my parentage, lots of people will rely upon me after my father retires. In a few short weeks Lady Eleanor will be my wife, and she will rely upon me too.

Rosie looked back at him steadily. "You loved me once," she said. "I don't care what you say. It was more than a kiss in the snow. It's as I have always said, men know nothing of real love."

"And what sort of world would it be," returned Jack stiffly, "if we all did exactly as we pleased instead of what is right? Forget about me Rosie Potter. You will return to London in the morning, to your house, to your market, to your adopted family, to your flower barrow ... and you will not think of me again."

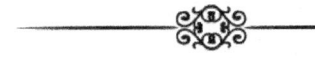

A young maid peeped suspiciously from Lady Eleanor's half opened front door. "What business have you at such a late hour?" she asked cheekily.

"It is John Beaumont," said Jack with authority, "And I wish to speak with Lady Eleanor if she is still up."

The maid, who had not recognised the visitors in the darkness was overcome with horror. She opened the door fully and proceeded to nod and curtsy. "I beg your pardon," she apologised. "We sometimes get ne'er-do-wells calling living as we do so close to the road." She cast Rosie a suspicious glance before leading the way into the lodge.

"Wait here," said Jack indicating that Rosie should be seated on the hall settle. "I will speak to Lady Eleanor first." Then he disappeared into the drawing room closing the door behind him so no conversation could be overheard.

After what seemed an eternity, Jack reappeared with Eleanor behind him. Eleanor was carrying a paraffin lamp, and the shadows jumped across the hall as the lamp's flame flickered and danced in the draft.

Eleanor descended upon Rosie and put her arm around her like an older sister. "Miss Potter," she said. "I hear you need a room and a change of clothes ahead of a long ride back to London in the morning." She waved her hand in the direction of her maid who was beginning to gawp at the realisation that Rosie was a young woman and not a teenage boy.

"Eliza," said Lady Eleanor handing her maid the paraffin lamp. "Show Miss Potter upstairs. Fill a ewer with some warm water for the guest room and show her my wardrobe. Miss Potter may choose anything from it she wishes to wear."

"And what am I to do with them boy's clothes?" asked Eliza scrunching her face in obvious disgust.

"Well they belong to Miss Potter," said Lady Eleanor gently, "and she may want to keep them. If she does not wish to keep them, we will wash and press them and pass them to the vicar the next time he calls for charity."

"Yes M'm," said Eliza casting Rosie another hostile look and she indicated with her head that Rosie should follow her up the stairs.

Rosie glanced miserably at Jack who had separated himself from the proceedings. He had moved back into Eleanor's drawing room and was standing looking down into the fireplace with his hands clasped firmly behind his back. Rosie felt a lump in her throat. This might be the very last time she would ever see him and yet he could not even look at her. This had not been the plan, yet it had been her only plan.

Eliza led the way to Lady Eleanor's bedroom. The rooms in the lodge had much lower ceilings than those in the hall itself, but the bedroom still afforded a four-poster bed and a double fronted oak carved wardrobe. Eliza set down the paraffin lamp and creaked open the wardrobe. "So who are you Miss Potter?" asked Eliza nosily. "You ain't no lady. You don't look like one or sound like one."

Rosie grinned. Eliza reminded her very much of herself. "I am not a liberty to say," she replied, "other than I sought to address a grave injustice but have failed. Your mistress," she added uncomfortably, "is very kind." Rosie looked down at her hands miserably. She would have preferred to have discovered that Lady Eleanor was haughty, unfeeling and remote. Instead she was discovering that Lady Eleanor was as kind and as warm as she was beautiful and poised.

Eliza lifted out some of the dresses from the wardrobes and laid them on bed. "If I was you," she said wistfully, "I would choose the blue silk with the embroidered bodice, or the yellow silk with the pearl buttoned cuffs."

Rosie ran her hand along the dresses and stopped at one in ivory lace.

"Would you like to see it?" asked Eliza with a knowing smile, and she lifted the dress from the wardrobe and laid it on the bed next to the blue silk. "This is my mistress's wedding dress. Beautiful ain't it? Can you picture what she will look like walking down the aisle in this?"

Rosie looked down at it and felt a gut-wrenching pain. Seeing the dress made the imminent wedding all the more inevitable. She tried to hate Jack for rejecting her, but she couldn't. She still loved him. She tried to tell herself that a marriage to Lady Eleanor could never work. But more and more she could see that everyone loved Lady Eleanor.

"Do you think that Lady Eleanor and John Beaumont are very much in love?" Rosie managed at last.

Eliza snorted. "You don't know much," she said. "The rich aren't like you or me." She unhitched another dress from its hook and held it up to the light so that the gold thread around its collar glittered. "The rich marry for titles, for money, for land and for property. They rarely marry for love."

Eliza chose another dress from the wardrobe. It was in a rich red velvet decorated in ruffles and ribbon. "I'd choose this one if I was you," she said.

Rosie stared sightlessly at the dress. "I'm not sure you answered my question," she said at last. "Do you think that Eleanor is very much in love?"

Eliza nodded. "Yes," she said. "I think she is very much in love." Then her face broke into a broad grin and her eyes twinkled. She lowered her voice. "But I do not think she is deeply in love with John Beaumont. Folks say she is in love with the vicar but that her family would not dream of allowing her to marry a clergy man."

Rosie's eyes shot wide. A littler flicker of hope was stirring. "But probably nothing more than a rumour do you not think? Folks will always gossip!"

"More than gossip," said Eliza pursing her mouth up disapprovingly. "The mistress goes over to the vicarage every week for a prayer meeting..." she paused for dramatic effect, "... without her prayer book!"

"Yes but..." Rosie scrunched her face up. "Forgetting one's prayer book is hardly evidence of a romantic liaison."

"And..." went on Eliza lowering her voice further still, "the mistress is forever over at the vicarage organising fetes and bazaars and charity dinners. What do you make of that?"

The flicker of hope burnt a little more strongly.

"But it is of no consequence," concluded Eliza fetching more dresses from the wardrobe. "Folks say that the mistress will marry into the Beaumont family because her family want the Beaumont land, and the Beaumont family will marry into the mistress's family because they need their fortune."

Rosie bit her lip. She picked the simplest dress of plain blue silk from the pile. "I should like this one," she said quietly.

Eliza's eyes widened in astonishment. "That old thing!" she said. "Of all the dresses you could have chosen; you have chosen the very one the mistress was about to give away to charity."

Rosie didn't sleep that night. She sat by the window of her small guest room watching the moon rise over the sprawling Beaumont estate. The crenellated silhouette of Beaumont Manor peeped from above the ancient oak trees. Rosie could see the flickering lights in the upper windows of the hall extinguished one by one as the inhabitants of the hall retired for the night. Rosie wondered if Jack was looking down from his window at Lady Eleanor's lodge. She wondered if he was giving Rosie Potter a second thought. Jack had chosen his path in life, and she couldn't deny that he had not swerved his duty to run the estate nor his moral obligation to protect his young sister from a wicked father. She could see now why discovering Jack's true parentage made no difference whatsoever. She leant her head against the latticed window. Why had she imagined that uncovering the family secret would free Jack from his duty and obligation? If anything, it had only strengthened it.

Dawn smudged the horizon with a streak of crimson. From the roadside of the lodge came the rhythmic clop and jangle of a horse and carriage. The oil lamps on either side of the driver's seat cast an eerie glow illuminating the long tunnel of oak trees beyond Beaumont's grand drive. With a sigh, Rosie knew this was the carriage Jack had organised to take her back to London.

If Rosie had imagined for one second that Jack would come down from the manor house to bid her farewell she was to be bitterly disappointed. The only person waiting for her at the gate was Eliza. Eliza handed Rosie a small basket neatly covered with a cloth. "I've made up some ham and egg rolls," explained the maid. "It's a long ride back to London."

Rosie took one last lingering look at Beaumont Manor. She gave one last thought of winning the heart of the man she had loved and lost.

"Farewell Miss Potter," said Eliza.

Chapter Nine

Ma' Maggie sat on the front pew of the church in her Sunday best. She wore a little blue velvet hat pinned carefully to hold it in place. She had put on a clean dress and had removed her apron which seemed odd, because without her apron Ma' Maggie simply didn't look like Ma' Maggie. Next to her sat Charlie, Will and Sparrow with their faces scrubbed and their boots polished. Rosie swallowed hard. It was good to be back in London and it was good to be with her little adopted family again. The boys had grown. They were looking healthy and strong and they were reading from their prayer books as though they had been reading all their lives.

The minister stepped up to the front and summoned Eddie, the doctor and his wife, Grace's brother-in-law who was to stand as Eddie's Godfather and Rosie to stand around the marble font.

"Dearly beloved," began the vicar. "None can enter into the kingdom of Heaven; except he be regenerated and born anew of water …." The vicar sprinkled water over Eddie's head, "I baptise thee Edward Blake."

Then Ma' Maggie and the boys burst into a boisterous rendition of, 'All things bright and beautiful all creatures great and small.'

There were smiles and hugs and kisses all round and then Grace invited everyone into the church hall for refreshments which was a suggestion met with huge excitement by the children. The boys ran ahead, and Eddie did his best to keep up, putting his best foot forward and expertly manipulating the brace on his other leg.

Rosie linked Ma' Maggie's arm companionably and helped her down the church steps. She watched Eddie striding along in the sunshine. She looked at the love in the faces of Dr Blake and his wife, and she thanked God that she was part of this family.

"I'm going to be the best Godmother to Eddie as ever a Godmother was," Rosie told Ma' Maggie. "Especially as…" she hesitated, "especially as I may never have children of my own."

"What nonsense!" snorted Ma' Maggie. "Of course you will have children of your own. She patted Rosie's hand. "Don't you worry Rosie Potter. Arthur Tipple was a wrong 'un, and happen Jack Beaumont is a wrong 'un too. But mark my words, another man will come along and sweep you off your feet."

Rosie took little consolation from this. She didn't want another man to sweep her off her feet. She only wanted Jack. "For the first time in my life," said Rosie. "I don't know what to do next." She gave a soft chuckle as she watched the boys race across the church hall and descend greedily on the cakes the doctor's wife had baked. "Except to keep an eye on these boys."

"Well I'll tell you what you're going to do next," said Ma' Maggie firmly. "You'll get up in the morning and bring flowers to market just as you've always done, and you and I shall keep each other company and make a little brass along the way just as we have always done."

Rosie smiled but it was a very wan sort of smile. She had hoped for so much more. Life she had learned was one disappointment after another. She looked up as the sun slanted in through the narrow church hall windows illuminating gently descending swirls of dust. She pulled herself up to her five foot four with new resolve. Ma' Maggie was right as she always was. She had no choice but to pick herself up and carry on the way she had always done. If life was full of disappointments it was full of opportunities too, and she would be sure to make the best of things.

Over the next days Rosie did what she had always done. She rose at five, collected flowers from the wholesalers and took them to market. Gradually, the customers who had thought she had gone for good began to trickle back. Just as she had always done, Rosie reverted easily to her old role, half flower seller half counsellor; advising the bereaved on what flowers to take to a funeral; advising the lovelorn on what flowers to give their intended.

It was late one afternoon that Rosie had some unexpected visitors. She had been making up a laurel funeral wreath when she had heard a gentle cough behind her and found Lady Eleanor waiting patiently for her attention. Rosie span round in surprise. Next to Lady Eleanor stood the Reverend Smythe, Beaumont's vicar.

"I'm sorry if we have startled you Miss Potter," said Lady Eleanor, "but we came on a matter of great sensitivity and we wonder if we might sit and talk for a while."

Rosie looked around for some barrels on which Lady Eleanor and the vicar could sit.

The vicar pointed to a little tea-room across the square. "Perhaps we could share a pot of tea," he suggested.

Rosie blushed furiously at the thought she had just been about to offer Lady Eleanor and the vicar barrels to sit on.

The vicar found the unlikely trio a table in the corner of the tearoom and ordered a pot of tea and a plate of spiced tea cakes.

"Is ... is Jack well?" asked Rosie suddenly fearing the worst. "John I mean."

"Yes John is well," smiled Eleanor, "but we fear..." she stopped in her tracks unable to find the right words.

"Miss Potter," said Reverend Smythe leaning across the table with his hands joined as though about to deliver a homily. "I believe that for everyone God has a plan. Do you believe that?"

Rosie hesitated. "I believe we are each born with talents," she said, "and it is up to us to discover our destiny."

Reverend Smythe's eyes lit up with something verging on triumph. "Exactly Miss Potter, exactly! For each of us God has a plan, and it is up to each of us to find out what that plan is. It is certainly not up to Leopold Fifth Earl of Beaumont to tell us what our destiny is."

Rosie looked from the vicar's earnest expression to Lady Eleanor's downcast and blushing face, and she struggled to conceal a smile. All at once she knew what this was about. She remembered how convinced Eliza had been, that Lady Eleanor and the Reverend Smythe were secretly in love. Was the vicar trying to free Eleanor from a marriage into the Beaumont family just as much as she had been trying to free Jack?

"So we have a plan Miss Potter," said Lady Eleanor, "and it involves you."

"We see the problem in Martha," said the vicar.

"Her father rules her with a rod of iron," put in Lady Eleanor.

"And as long as the earl has jurisdiction over the child," said the vicar, "everyone else has to do his bidding."

"All of us fear for the child's welfare," went on Eleanor her face crumpled with concern.

"But nothing can change that," said Rosie who had already given the matter much thought. "Nothing can change that Leopold is Martha's father and that he can make decisions over her future and the future of Beaumont."

"But perhaps there is a way," said the vicar. He took a letter from his pocket and pushed it across the table for Rosie to read.

Rosie read the letter slowly, skipping the more difficult words and hoping she was understanding it correctly.

Sensing that Rosie had never had the privilege of an education, Eleanor explained the letter. "Reverend Smythe has a good friend; Lord Clancy. Lord Clancy is a lawyer, and he believes that if we can prove that Leopold is unfit to bring up his daughter, then we can present a case at the Court of Chancery in London to transfer guardianship of Martha to her brother John."

Rosie looked from the vicar's determined face to Lady Eleanor's hopeful face and her heart began to pound.

"But we need your help," said Lady Eleanor. "We need to prove first what a cruel father he was to John."

"We heard about the letters you found," said the vicar. "We need to know where you found them and where they are now. The letters are proof that Leopold has a brother, George. We believe those letters hold much evidence. Evidence of how Leopold's brother and his wife Dorothea handed their baby John into the care of Leopold and of Mary who at the time were struggling to conceive a child of her own. Evidence that John was treated cruelly by Leopold, and that Mary did little to protect the child."

"We have spoken with George and Dorothea," said Eleanor gently. "It was their belief that they were doing the right thing in giving away their child. George was the rightful fifth earl, but he renounced his position to marry beneath his status. Dorothea was a seamstress."

"But why couldn't they keep their baby?" asked Rosie hotly. She was beginning to see how differently Jack's life might have been if he had grown up with parents who had loved him instead of Mary who had been remote and Leopold who had been cruel and never shown the boy any love.

"Out of a misguided sense of kindness," said Eleanor shaking her head sadly. "Dorothea was sorry for Mary who at the time could not conceive. More importantly, she believed that although her husband had renounced his title, John should not be denied his entitlement as the sixth earl. Once John was legally adopted, he would be the rightful heir."

"It suited Leopold too," said Reverend Smythe. "He was keen to have a son who could continue the Beaumont lineage and run the estate."

"So George and Dorothea gave away their baby and allowed Mary and Leopold to adopt for title and lineage," finished Rosie bitterly.

"Do not judge them too harshly," said Eleanor. "They were not to know how much the boy would be ill-treated."

"So now we need the evidence," said Reverend Smythe, and Rosie could see by the glint in his eye that this was a personal mission for the vicar. "We need to know how we can find those letters. Miss Potter, we need your testimony word for word of the night Leopold broke into your house and threatened that if John refused to return to Beaumont he would cut off his inheritance and marry off his twelve-year-old sister to ensure financial security for the estate."

Lady Eleanor poured more tea and added lemon. She was looking flushed. "Then," she said, "we need to prove that just as Leopold was unfit to bring up his adopted son, he was equally unfit to bring up his daughter."

Rosie nodded thoughtfully. "The servants say they rarely see Martha," she said. "It is as though she is kept a prisoner in her own room."

"So you will help us Miss Potter?" asked Eleanor.

Rosie imagined the years Leopold had subjected the young Jack and Martha to his tyranny and cruelty and she dug her fingernails into her palms. She detested bullies. Bullies came in all shapes and sizes. Leopold Beaumont was no better than Morgan Heneghan in fine robes.

Rosie stuck out her chin. "Of course I'll help," she said. "I can tell you exactly how to find the letters. I can certainly remember word for word Leopold's visit to my home, and I can make a list of all the other servants at Beaumont who can bear witness to bullying and beatings. And of course, I will stand witness myself. I have no fear of facing Leopold Beaumont across the Court of Chancery.

A thick fog rolled in from the river stinging Rosie's eyes and filling her nose with an acrid stench. She pulled her shawl tighter and for the umpteenth time untied and retied the ribbons on the bonnet she was so unused to wearing.

She crossed the courtyard to the Court of Chancery hoping she appeared braver than she felt. The Old Hall rose ahead of her, its pinnacles and steep roof shrouded in the descending gloom. Carriages were pulling up at the grand entrance their lamps lit as though it were night. People were emerging all around her like ghosts. As she grew nearer, she began to recognise faces. She recognised servants from Beaumont some looking determined to present their case and others looking terrified. She saw Martha with a chaperone. She looked small for her twelve years of age, her face pinched and white. She spotted Reverend Smythe helping Lady Eleanor down from her carriage. Lady Eleanor gave Rosie a wave and a reassuring nod of her head. As the solemn crowd moved through the grand entrance to the court, Rosie's eyes scanned the benches for Jack, but she could not see any sign of him.

The court room was full, and Rosie felt a flutter of nerves. She would rather face the Heneghan brothers across the market any day than speak in front of all these people. Presiding over proceedings was the Lord High Chancellor who sat wigged and cloaked on a dais high above everybody else. Below him, at a long-polished table sat the Master of Rolls and a team of clerks, quills at the ready. On three sides of the court were tiered benches. In the front bench sat Martha between her chaperone on the left and Lady Eleanor on her right. At the back sat a huddle of newspaper reporters, pencils and notepads ready for what they hoped would make them a front-page story.

"Call Rosie Potter," cried a clerk, and Rosie made her way to the front of the courtroom. Her heart skipped a beat. She had spotted Jack. He was wearing a charcoal suit and fine silk cravat. He was sitting very upright and staring stonily ahead looking neither to his left nor his right. Leopold sat on the other side of the court looking even more dour than usual. His gaze swept over Rosie as though daring her to give evidence against him.

Lord Clancy, who was standing before the chancellor gave Rosie an encouraging smile. "Tell us in your own words Miss Potter about the day Leopold Beaumont called at your house, and the events that followed."

Rosie began hesitantly. She described how Leopold had entered her house uninvited and how he had revealed that the man she had thought was homeless and down on his luck was in fact the earl's son disguised as a beggar to escape his father. She described how the earl had blackmailed Jack into returning to Beaumont by threatening to marry off Martha as a twelve-year-old child bride to a man who would run the estate in Jack's place. When she got to the part of the story where she had dressed up as a garden boy to infiltrate Beaumont and discover the family secrets in an effort to free Jack from his father there were gasps of astonishment from the benches and the newspaper reporters scribbled all the faster. Was it Rosie's imagination or did Jack's mouth twitch very slightly when she described how she had sneaked into Mary Beaumont's bedroom and discovered the letters and diaries that revealed Jack's true parentage and which had told how cruelly he had been brought up.

At this point the earl leapt to his feet in a fury. "I object to this 'so called' evidence," he roared. "The girl has trespassed and deceived. She is nothing but a common fraudster. How can you believe a single word that comes out of her mouth? If you listen to one more word of her lies, I shall prosecute her for trespass in my home, more specifically, my dead wife's room."

Lord Clancy raised one eyebrow. "Sir are you sure you want to do that?" he asked. "Did you yourself not break a window to unlock a door and let yourself uninvited into Miss Potter's home?"

Leopold collapsed back into his chair his face as black as thunder. A ripple of giggles and gasps spread across the benches.

Lord Clancy turned to Rosie with a slight smile. "That will be all Miss Potter. You are free to leave."

Rosie left the court her mind racing. She wondered if she had said everything there had been to say. She wondered if she had said it well enough. Martha and Jack's futures depended upon it.

As she reached the grand entrance and descended back out onto the courtyard, Reverend Smythe caught her up. He took her hand and shook it. "Well done Miss Potter," he said. "Very well done indeed."

"When will we know the verdict?" asked Rosie.

The vicar gestured that this was in the lap of the gods. "There will probably be no decision today," he said, "nor tomorrow or even the day after. This court is renowned for drawing things out."

Rosie's eyes shot wide in horror. "But surely it is clear that the earl is unfit to bring Martha up!"

The vicar patted her hand. "The longer the court spins out the proceedings, the more money they will be paid. It is the way of the world Miss Potter."

Rosie was disconsolate. She had been naive to expect an immediate verdict. She tried to be patient but the fates of Jack and of young Martha were constantly on her mind. Every day she walked by the paper man who hollered out the front-page stories, but there was no news of a verdict on the ongoing court case.

Days and weeks passed by, and the case dragged on. Rosie's spirits began to plummet. She had thought the case was cut and dried, but it was appearing not to be. And the longer that the case dragged on, the more Rosie feared for Martha. She dreaded to think how Leopold would treat his daughter if Jack lost his petition. Misery washed over her. If Jack lost his case she would never see him again. The flicker of hope the case had ignited began to ebb.

Ma' Maggie gave up on giving words of comfort and took to singing cheery songs to keep Rosie's spirits up. "I'll sing you a good old song," she sang, "made by a good old pate, of a fine old English gentleman who had an old estate…" Then she took to hitching up her skirts and dancing around her barrow, "…and who kept up his old mansion at a bountiful old rate…" A few intrigued passers-by stopped to watch her dance and sing. They laughed and clapped. Despite herself, Rosie began to smile. Ma' Maggie had always been her role model. Ma' Maggie had taught her resilience and defiance in the face of every adversity. Without resilience, what else did women like Rosie and Ma' Maggie have?

Rosie's lips began to move. She began to join in the song. " …With a good old porter to relieve, the old poor at his gate."

Then a man's voice, deep and resonant joined in the chorus. "Like a fine old English gentleman, one of the olden time…"

Rosie and Ma' Maggie looked up in surprise. They recognised the voice instantly.

"Jack!" mouthed Ma' Maggie. "Well if it isn't the prodigal son!"

Jack inclined his head and gestured apology. "Forgive me for not coming sooner," he said. "It's a fleeting visit. I've come straight from the court. You were the first people I had to tell." He spoke quickly as though aware of how much Rosie had been suffering. "The chancellor has reached a decision." He allowed himself a brief smile. "We won! I have sole guardianship of my sister. She is safe."

Ma' Maggie gave a shriek of delight. She leapt up and gave him a hug. "So now you'll be free to marry our Rosie!" she cried.

Jack's smile faded and looked suddenly solemn. "As I said," he faltered, "this is a fleeting visit. There is much to do. Forgive me if I take my leave. I will return." And with that he tipped his hat at Rosie and strode off.

Rosie coloured puce. "Ma' Maggie," she snapped. "What on earth possessed you to say that? You embarrassed me deeply and you clearly embarrassed Jack too."

"Garn!" laughed Ma' Maggie flapping her hands dismissively. "There's no embarrassing Jack Beaumont." And she went about shovelling chestnuts into paper cones totally unrepentant.

The day wore on. Rosie distractedly wired forget-me-nots and lavender into endless posies far more than she was likely to sell. Jack had said that he would return. Had he meant it? His life had changed. Not only did he have responsibility for the Beaumont estate, but now for his twelve-year-old sister too. How was it now possible for him to marry a lowly flower girl? How was it possible for him to introduce a girl who had pushed a barrow to market for most of her working life into high society? It was clearly impossible.

The sun came down on the market. Rosie counted her takings. She had earned very little that day.

"Cheer up ducks!" cackled Ma' Maggie. "Jack will be back. I feel it in my waters."

Chapter Ten

The gas light that overlooked Rosie's back yard illuminated rods of icy rain. Rosie rooted through her bunker for some lumps of coal. She found five lumps of coal, a lot of coal dust and a piece of wood which was damp and would most likely smoke. It was better than nothing. She filled a scuttle and went into the house which was dark and cold. She lit a small fire and a single candle, then she cut up some bread and heated some potato soup. It was a far cry from the days Jack had kept the bunker full of coal and brought beef home as a treat.

As Rosie ate she could hear the sounds of evening revellers making their way to and from the tavern on the corner of the street. The sound was comforting. She was part of the local community she told herself. Everybody in the market knew and valued her. She had her little adopted family who loved her and a Godson who would always look to her example. She had everything she needed she told herself. She didn't need Jack Beaumont. She didn't, she told herself, need any man.

One of the passers-by seemed to stop at her window and glance in. Rosie paused with a spoonful of soup suspended halfway to her lips. Then there was a gentle tap on the door. It was Jack! Rosie dropped her spoon and went to let him in. She tried not to run, but there was a skip in her step. He stood looking down at her waiting to be invited across the threshold. His face was uncharacteristically nervous. He was bearing the largest bouquet of roses she had ever seen in her whole life.

"Roses!" Rosie looked up at him with a mixture of incomprehension and trepidation. She couldn't allow herself to believe their message of love. Men, as she had always maintained, had no understanding of real love. She had spent her working life selling the language of flowers, yet suddenly that language was ambiguous. Could the roses be saying something else? Could they be speaking of consolation or apology?

"For you!" said Jack pressing the bouquet into her arms.

"But roses?" she repeated hesitating to accept them. She stood looking down at the little red heads whose fragile petals trembled in the cold night air.

"May I come in?" asked Jack, and she stood aside to allow him in.

Without waiting to be asked, Jack sat in his old chair and set his top hat to one side.

"Would you like some potato soup?" was all Rosie could think of to say.

"If there is enough?" said Jack. "I can't remember the last time I ate."

So Rosie filled a second bowl, and they sat in companionable silence or a moment or two whilst the modest fire spat and smoked. She looked up at him shyly. Apart from his aristocratic garb, this was the way things had once been.

"I wish..." said Rosie, "...I wish things were as they were before," she managed at last. "I wish we were back in the days where I didn't have to count the lumps of coal. I wish we were back in the days where we could eat beef and afford a window cleaner. I wish we were at this table once more making wreaths for Christmas. I wish we were back at the market, you and me and our little adopted family. I wish you were plain old Jack once more and not John Beaumont." She put down her spoon. She suddenly had no appetite. She looked up into his face which suddenly seemed full of pity. It was the last expression she wanted to see. "I don't suppose..." she struggled with a fantasy. "I don't suppose we could put the clock back."

"What are you proposing Rosie Potter?" asked Jack cocking his head on one side.

"I wonder if you might move back in," said Rosie.

"And live in your stable loft?" said Jack with a low chuckle.

Rosie closed her eyes. "I'm sorry!" she said. "I hardly know what I am saying. I know of course that we cannot put the clock back. I know that you are not Jack. You are John Beaumont and one day you will be the Sixth Earl of Beaumont. I know that you are responsible for the upbringing of your twelve-year-old sister. I know that there is no place in your life for a barrow girl."

Jack finished his soup and considered her for a moment. "You told me to go and seek out Dorothea and George," he said, "and so I did. I knew as soon as I looked upon Dorothea that she was my real mother. She took me in her arms. She cried. She told me that not a day had passed when she had regretted the decision to give me up for adoption by Mary and Leopold. I cannot tell you how good it felt to have my mother's arms around me. My real mother!" Jack reached across the table and took Rosie's hands in his. His hands were steady and reassuring. "My father spoke of his regret too at having given me up to a brother who had acted only out of self interest and never out of kindness."

"You mustn't judge Dorothea and George too harshly," said Rosie repeating Lady Eleanor's words. "They did what they thought was best."

"George taught me a lesson," said Jack softly. "He married Dorothea out of love, and he loves her now as much as he did when she was just a seamstress in a village shop. Marrying Dorothea was the best decision he ever made. But when he decided out of a misguided sense of duty to renounce his title and estate in favour of Leopold, well that was the very worst decision he could have made." Jack tightened his hold on Rosie's hand. "Rosie Potter," he said. "Do you hear what I am saying? Decisions made from love can never be wrong."

Rosie pulled her hand away uncertainly. She didn't know what he was suggesting. She picked up the bouquet that she had set to one side. "I'll put these in a vase," she said, and she took them into the scullery.

Jack followed her. "I have something for you," he said. The space in the scullery was small, and he was standing so close to her that she could feel his breath on her forehead. He took a ring from his pocket and slid it onto her engagement finger. "Rosie Potter come back to Beaumont Manor as my wife. Marry me Rosie."

Rosie's world swam. She gaped at the ring as though unable to comprehend. She remembered the time Arthur Tipple had slid an engagement ring onto her finger. She remembered the little brass ring with its paste diamond which in the fullness of time, had spoken of nothing but lies and false promises. This ring with its twinkling diamonds was different. It was genuine.

But still Rosie couldn't allow herself to believe in a happy-ever-after. "What about the earl?" she asked quickly. "He will never accept me."

"He has left on a sojourn to India to check his financial interests there," said Jack. "In truth, he has gone to lick his wounds. If and when he returns, he will find that everything is different. I will be there to run the estate just as he wished. I will be there to continue his lineage as was always his ambition, but it will be on my terms not his."

Rosie continued to look down at the diamond setting that glittered in the light of the streetlamp that shone through the little scullery window. A sudden thought twisted in her gut. Had he given Eleanor an engagement ring too? "And what of Lady Eleanor?" she asked with a sudden frown. "What of the wedding that everyone is expecting?"

"It is common knowledge that she loves another," he replied with a slight smile. "Rosie," he said as though she deserved more explanation than this. "Eleanor and I have known each other since childhood. We are like brother and sister. Nothing more. She has no more wish to marry me than I have to marry her. I promise you that."

Rosie shook her head. "I will never fit in," she said. "A barrow girl with rough manners and no education."

"But Rosie," said Jack, "you had already won the hearts and minds of everyone at Beaumont. The head gardener tells me of all the wonderful ideas you had for the greenhouses and gardens and how we could develop Beaumont's business interests." He gave a low chuckle. "Just think how much more influence you would have as Lady Rose Beaumont than a grubby gardener's boy."

Rosie's breath caught in her throat. She allowed herself to believe she could have a purpose at Beaumont. She allowed herself to believe that she and Jack could be happy there.

"Rosie," said Jack, "and his voice was ragged. "Don't make me suffer any longer. Give me your decision."

Rosie looked up into his face. "Yes," she said. "Yes I will marry you."

Jack folded his arms around her. He pulled her close and kissed the top of her head. "You have made me the happiest man," he said and kissed her cheeks and eyelids.

"I wonder if I shall ever feel like Lady Rose Beaumont though," she said enjoying the warmth and firmness of his body. "I will always be Rosie Potter."

"And I," he said kissing her hard on the lips, "will always be Jack."

She kissed him back with a passion and an excitement that surged through her body and overtook her senses.

His hands ran feverishly over her slender body. She didn't stop him. "I love you Rosie Potter," he said. He started to laugh. "I think I loved you from that very first day I saw you swing a hot griddle at Morgan Heneghan."

Rosie nestled her cheek into the arch of his neck where she could hear his pulse racing. It had always been her opinion that men knew little of true love. Perhaps she had been wrong.

The wedding took place in Beaumont's rose garden. To get married in a darkened chapel didn't feel the right setting for Jack and his flower girl bride. The staff had been given the promise of an extra day's holiday to celebrate the occasion. The lawn had been arranged with rows of benches and chairs for everyone to witness the special day and a marquee had been erected to house the refreshments. A small quartet of musicians were tuning up and Reverend Smythe, who was to preside over the wedding was putting his notes in order.

Rosie had arrived a week prior to the wedding. Dorothea had volunteered to make Rosie's wedding dress and had worked day and night to get it finished. The result was a narrow waisted dress in fine silk, satin and taffeta, with a long train.

"If I'd have had more time," said Dorothea with regret, "I would have embroidered the bodice. I wish that John had not been in such a hurry to marry."

Rosie had smiled. "It is the most beautiful dress I have ever seen," she had said. "I can't quite believe that I will be wearing it." Then she had given her mother-in-law to be a quick hug. She had very quickly developed an affection for Jack's real parents with their genuine expressions of kindness and humility.

Then Ma' Maggie had arrived a day before the wedding followed by Sparrow, Eddie, Charlie and Will. Jack had insisted on putting them all up at the manor house and the servants were treating them as though they were aristocracy. The servants carefully concealed half-shocked grins as they boys tore around the house and slid down the magnificent bannisters. Martha had stood and watched from a safe distance. She had never observed how children her own age were supposed to behave. Will and Charlie with no sense of restraint or impropriety had spotted her standing by shyly and dragged her into the game.

"What! You never slid down a bannister before?" cried Will in astonishment.

"It's easy miss," said Charlie. "Hitch up your petticoats and climb on... like this..." he demonstrated how to climb onto the bannister.

Martha had wobbled dangerously.

"And hold on tight!" warned the boys.

"Push off gently..." Will had advised from the top of the grand staircase as Charlie and Martha had shot off down the well of the house far too fast.

"Oh... and don't forget to hop off at the bottom!" cried Will as they all landed in a heap with squeals of laughter.

Without Leopold, the house already felt very different. The atmosphere of tyranny and oppression lifted to be replaced with an atmosphere where anyone whether they were part of the Beaumont family, a servant or a tenant could flourish and thrive like green shoots in a new springtime.

Meanwhile Ma' Maggie sat and observed everything and everyone like a wise old grandmother. She had refused to sit in the grand drawing room and chosen to sit instead in the kitchen helping Molly to peel potatoes.

Rosie had sat by her side. "I fear it will be lonely for you back in London now that we have all gone our different ways," she had said her face crumpled with concern. "Jack says there will always be a place for you here if you wish."

Ma' Maggie had thrown back her head and cackled as though it was the best joke she had ever heard. "What me? Here at Beaumont? Lawks! I'd be like one of Ed's eels out of water. Don't worry about me Rosie Potter. The market is where I belong, and I'll never be far away."

"In that case," Rosie had slid a small envelope from her pocket and pressed it into Ma' Maggie's hand. "This is a small gift from Jack to you."

"What for me! Never had a present before!" she said tearing open the envelope.

"It's a barrow licence," Rosie had grinned. "You need never be afraid of the Heneghan brothers again.

Ma' Maggie had thrown back her head and cackled all the more. "Can't wait until I meet the Heneghan brothers again, what with me on the right side of the law and them what definitely ain't!"

Reverend Smythe cleared his throat "Dearly beloved, we are gathered together here in the sight of God, and in the face of this congregation, to join together this man and this woman in holy matrimony...."

Rosie looked around the congregation all seated in the sunshine. Above them the climbing roses in the arbours nodded their heads and dropped their petals in the breeze like confetti. She glanced at Jack's profile and her heart welled. She hardly dared to be this happy.

The vicar opened his homily notes. Those who were used to the Reverend Smythe's homilies exchanged weary glances. The vicar was renowned for his very long and deeply theological homilies which were above the heads of most.

"Beloved brethren, and especially you, the man and woman before us," began Reverend Smythe with the air of a man with another twenty-three pages to read, ".... entering into this sacred union, permit me to expound upon the profound mystery of matrimony as it is intertwined with the very fabric of divine ordinance and eternal truth..."

The children on the front row began to fidget and pinch each other. Faces began to glaze. "Consider, if you will, the typology of Adam and Eve," continued the vicar. The congregation began to wilt. Even the roses on their stems appeared to wilt. Only Lady Eleanor hung on Reverend Smythe's every word.

Then from nowhere the vicar's homily was rudely interrupted by a series of high-pitched, sharp chirps. It was a bright and cheerful call, but it was loud and insistent. The congregation twisted their heads to spot the offending bird.

"I apologise!" said the vicar as though a noisy bird might in some way be his fault. He halted his homily and waited for the bird to stop. It didn't. "I do believe it sounds like a love bird," he said, his face crumpled in puzzlement. "But how can that be? Love birds in this country only live in captivity."

Rosie was suddenly suspicious. She spun round and caught Sparrow's face. His face was cheekily puckered up in one of his famous bird calls. Other congregation members spotted him too. Someone began to laugh, then everyone began to laugh. Rosie gave Sparrow a stern look which demanded that he stop, and with a good-natured grin he obliged.

"Now, where was I?" said the Reverend Smythe sifting through his notes.

"Skip to the vows vicar!" called Ma' Maggie irreverently and there was another ripple of laughter.

A little disconcerted, the vicar skipped to the vows and, "... You may now kiss the bride."

There were whoops and cheers as Jack raised Rosie's veil and kissed her very tenderly. The string quartet broke into an uplifting rendition of "La Rejouissance", and Martha scooped up handfuls of rose petals and threw them over the newlyweds.

"Rosie, I hope you will be happy at Beaumont," said Jack withdrawing from the kiss with a sudden look of concern. "I've taken you away from everything you know and value most."

Rosie looked up at him with mock severity. "Jack Beaumont," she said. "It is true. You have taken me away from everything I've ever loved," Then she reached up and returned his kiss. "But what I love most and will ever love most ... is right here."

A Note From The Author

If you enjoyed this book, please take a minute to leave a good review on the website from which you bought it. This will help me to write and sell more books.

Thank you

Printed in Great Britain
by Amazon